About the author

I was born in Hackney, London in 1984. I grew up in Glastonbury. In Autumn 1996 my family and I relocated to Cambridge. There I completed my studies at Hills Road Sixth Form College and then went to Liverpool University to complete my BA in Music and Media.

I was a nationally published poet as a child. At seventeen I was internationally published. Songwriting led to my forming a band in Cambridge and the limitations of poetical and lyrical verse caused me to begin to write *The Religion of Self-Enlightenment.*

D1342347

The Religion of
Self-Enlightenment

The Religion of
Self-Enlightenment

Emily Scialom

The Religion of Self-Enlightenment

Olympia Publishers
London

www.olympiapublishers.com
OLYMPIA PAPERBACK EDITION

A CIP catalogue record for this title is
available from the British Library.

ISBN: 978-1-84897-753-2

First Published in 2016

Olympia Publishers
60 Cannon Street
London
EC4N 6NP

Printed in Great Britain

Dedication

To you.

Acknowledgments

Love and sincere gratitude to those who supported me throughout the process of producing *The Religion of Self-Enlightenment: Michael Scialom, Florence Scialom, Charlie Baker, Frances Anagnostou, Kostas Anagnostou, Yanni Anagnostou, Sophia Anagnostou, Julia Travers-Wakeford, Mark Offord, Alison Dymond, Lucy Chima, Akash Chima, Owen Martindell, Tom Martindell, Aggie Andrews, Jaine Raine, Andy Bow, Mathijs Ruisch, Christine Bartram, Luci Lucas, Maria Xoubanova, Julia Lis, Danny Delgado Rosas, Helen Russ, Layla Smyth, Deneen Holohan, Wesley Freeman-Smith, Seonaid Kay, Emma-Rose Cornwall, Rufus Fox, Thom Dobbin, Nancy Peters, Kit Peters, Sam Peters, Molly Peters, Christy Rowell, Guy Johnson, Geri Darrington, Hannah Dunleavy, Matt Smith, Matt Cope, Muhammad Chilwan, Victoria Goldsmith, Vivienne Goldsmith, Bartholemew Ullstein, Olympia Publishers.*

ONE

He was the kind of person who has forgotten why he is here. He was boring, and proudly so. Every ounce of ingredients the world had thrown at Carrick Ares had been thrown onwards into his life's oven. The result was horrific, of course – just not to Other People. Yet because this was a segment of Carrick's reality whose opinions he courted fiercely, he almost managed to sustain the impression that he was that death-of-all-deaths: okay. "How are you?" they would say. "I'm okay", he would reply. But there was no reason for this, because in truth Carrick could never be anything other than extraordinary. And there was never a single, dreary, rain-soaked moment of his life in which he could possibly reduce himself to the depths of being merely 'okay'.

If Carrick had his way with how you saw him, if he could really orchestrate your mind, he would make you believe the idea of understanding him to be something of excruciating pain. This was a measure aiming to prevent people from becoming close to him. For when the sun rose, he would make a conscious decision to reveal nothing that it could not shine upon. He sometimes lost himself in sadness, but aside from these lapses of raw, choking sorrow, he was fine – drained of emotion and devoid of desire – but fine. He understood that this is how you should live. He had seen it in the newspaper and in the eyes and words of the people he met: images of war and rape, the violent condemnation for violent acts, the hatred of who we really and genuinely are.

As a result he had grown afraid and learned to disdain and strongly doubt anything besides that which he had been told by other people. Acquiescence was his shield against the violence he felt surrounded by. If ever a situation arose, complex and nuanced, which required more of him than to be an incarnate reiteration he simply learned more things to repeat. And did so with an added passion: he had no idea of what it was to be original, to exist.

Yet like most of Carrick's highest dreams about himself, the desire to be impenetrable to others was a hopeless self-deceit: for Carrick Ares was a total phenomenon. In truth, he could be anything he chose to be.

Yet he pretended not to know this.

It became clear, after a while, that courting ignorance was not clever. He reached the point in early adulthood by which the buried accumulation of thoughts he'd been unwilling to think about had gathered and joined into vast tectonic plates beneath the surface of his world. They grew steadily and rubbed against one another daily. And without heed of his desire or any warning provided, they would erupt. He would be out in the most peaceful of settings and it would happen: that which he was seeing, hearing, touching or tasting would suddenly dissolve into the background, while to the foreground burst screaming, violent visions of what he wanted to be, what was unfulfilled in himself, and how far he was from these things. He would cry and tell himself, "It's natural to feel this way". Yet it was a lie he could barely contain along with all the others – it was just something he had heard and repeated without hesitation. He cried again at what he had been given to quieten himself with, because yes, it was clear to all who knew him that the soul within him had much emotion. He just did not know how to express it, had not been told how.

In contrast to what might be expected in such circumstances, Carrick was no man of faith (thank God). Yet neither was he a man of no faith (poor souls). No, he was a man of the curiously strange times in which he was living; he had simply never really thought about being either.

He would say that his total lack of convictions was a terrible consequence of the way he was never allowed time to discern his beliefs in the mad rush for money and power... to some people. To others, he would expatiate heartily about how anyone who believes that they can use recycled, disingenuous beliefs that have no doubt been held by millions of others throughout history is severely delusional. You see, that was his way. He was neither liberal nor conservative, a paper-chaser or a charity-giver, a good man or a bad man: he was all of them, and would decide which part of his wondrous personality to show according to whom he was with and what they would approve of most.

You may find this appalling, yet Carrick knew it was inevitable: the value the world places on truth is the most hypocritical of all human ideals. People make it very clear, even to each other, that they do not value truth: they just claim to. In Carrick's playful, blindfolded way, he was therefore practising a very high degree of awareness. For taken at their root source, these attitudes postulated a much higher ideal: to be everything was their ultimate aim – and that means lies, and lots of them. The truth was that Carrick spent his whole life trying to avoid looking his opinions in the face – just in case he recognised one that someone might disapprove of. Again, one is taught to condemn such attitudes. But Carrick was wise and aware. He had a strong sense that in life, merely by breathing, it is often the case that one incites enough hatred to break a heart in two. And so it was somehow unwise to provoke any more antagonism through the incubation of the still-born opinions of people who, if they should have ever met, would have hated him in their turn.

Yet do not take all this at face value. It is the portrait of a man of deception, and who knows what you will see in Carrick by the end. The question to be asked at the beginning, however, is not what he had become by the time of his death but what he was in spite of death. And the point to be seen clearest of all is that whatever anyone else saw in the Carrick of that time, Carrick himself could never see his true self.

As for the company he kept, in terms of unconditional love, Carrick's girlfriend Beth – who claimed the affections of many others – was the proud, sole flower in a bed of weeds. They had been together for almost two years, a long time for Carrick, who had treated his previous partners badly. At twenty-nine years old, he was past the confusion of youth, but still felt its lingering consequences. In his younger days, he had gotten himself into quite a muddle over the basics of his genitals and where to put them, as most do; "It looks wrong, it is uncontrollable; it wants men, it wants women, it wants nothing; what is going on?" and walked around with a cyclone in his head for years. Family, friends and lovers were bruised and contorted inside it.

Beth, however, had a mental biography which read not at all like his. She was a lot more stable and single-minded, and the power she had over her thoughts was a gift which Carrick knelt before, as at a secret inner altar, longing as he was for such a blessing in his own life. They had met in a park on one of those sunny days that never draws breath, and her smile had been silly as she kept kicking a football against a hedge when she had been aiming for a lamppost. Three weeks later, Beth and Carrick were lovers, and two days after that Carrick found himself having his inane post-sex banter rudely disturbed by Beth's serious questions. She actually wanted to know Carrick. Really know him. This scared Carrick immediately, for he knew he had no answer to the question of who he was.

On a deceptively still night she lay, naked as the baby she basically was, and touched him in a way he could not begin to reciprocate. She moved like she didn't have to, and liked to be the things he had so long ago abandoned; exposed and recklessly thoughtful. She became deeply embarrassed when he tried to make her crude and vulgar, wanting to reach a destination beyond a distraction from what had gone before. Her conversation flowed in ways his was dammed, and he felt nothing except hopeless when he tried to swim in its powerful currents. He was intimidated by the raven's eyes she had which looked kind but never shied away from him. They wasted time together trying to find his more interesting thoughts and make them dull. She had a habit of doing this, of taking something strange and unheard and making it understandable. She would hear it.

He would lose himself in tantrums of abandonment when alone, even when she left his side for one unjustified second! He would lean against a wall, anguishing over the details that had somehow passed him by when they had first occurred and then as he recalled them later would stir him in a deep place for which he had no map. He grew volatile and cared for her, in spite of his defences. He smoked mountains of cigarettes and drank gallons of alcohol, tied to depression as a prisoner to something sharp. He would damage himself with thoughts of her before she had a chance to damage anyone at all. He tried to tire of her before she could return one time, so he did not have to bare her anymore, his thoughts a lust within the body of the mind. He was just so enraged that she had been born as herself and not him, and would ask himself seriously why no one had ever noticed the justice of this situation.

After half of another Tuesday wasting his energies, he refused to see her, thus introducing a fateful night which would not go unnoticed. He gazed out towards the sun, and a sky was before him which he instantly recognized as the same sky he had dreamt of when he was a child.

When he was a young boy he would regularly visit the seaside towns of Cornwall. The towns always had at least one cliff in close proximity that provided a view that was impossible to capture with paints. He would sit for hours and admire it. He felt himself to be an active dreamer in a dream of the world. He watched as the birds and the waves played, saw them end with a blur of his failed vision. But then a sky began to become visible. He understood all there was in life as he saw it passing in processions of divine inconclusiveness.

He would think of Biblical adventures that he heard. Moses had parted the Red Sea with only his passionate desire and the help of a Lord that the young Carrick thought almost nothing about. He realised that there is a reward received for putting faith in desire. 'DESIRE!' He then said out loud to the world. 'WHAT CAN IT DO?'

He would have looked back and forth from sky to ocean again were his blue eyes open. Yet he was looking to keep a part of gleams or rhythms that he had sensed for himself, through making memories which could be attached to his mind. Desire was his now. He wished to remain upon its throne. Yet instead he had to work alongside it to be a part of its wonder. Time would teach him this as he listened to its messages.

Then he thought of the way in which no one had moved the skies as Moses had moved the sea, and he declared that he was going to be the one who did.

The dreams of that time long hidden by various sedimentary layers, little could he have foreseen that one had been seeking the right time for it to manifest. It was seemingly gathering the necessary desperation that permits dreams to be realised.

When he watched the sky years later as an adult and a dream-stealer, it indeed began to realise itself before him. To look at it as a stranger one would not fail to see how strangely the sky appeared. It was as if God was drawing a line slowly from behind Carrick's head to the furthest point on the horizon, and then began to push away the cloud on either side of the line. It was exactly as he had imagined it to be. He told himself that it was not by his hand, but a sense of disorientation and elation began to grow within his soul.

It felt like the divisions that existed previously between reality and dreams were now non-existent. The clouds of inquisition which had been covering his feelings towards Beth also changed, and the dream that was fuelled by a sense of immense desire and desperation then was clearly manifested: he was in love.

TWO

Disappointment has a way of playing havoc with the memory: despair becomes dissipated by the distortion and ingenuous cruelty toward pasts which hold no worth except in their ability to derange a person. But Carrick's past with Beth was to become something absolutely blessed. She had passed the towering watch-guards of his privacy, and stolen from his prison the idea that there was anything interesting about him at all. As a shining thief then, she played games with him like they were children, laughing in the sun because they knew they had no idea about any of the rules, and had forgotten the purpose of their lives except simply to enjoy one another's company. It was heaven. They sang to each other in quiet and emotive tones, shy to raise their voices to the full extent of their talent-less din: 'Limitless, undying love…'

All his life Carrick Philip Ares had been very ordinary. He had a mother who cooked well, a father who worked well, and a sister who studied well. He got along with them fairly well, as did they with one another.

As a child he had always got what he wanted for Christmas, and was especially fond of the flame-coloured Mustang which he rode everywhere, and his puppy, Prince. (If Heaven were a person, and so happy that she cried, the teardrop shed would encapsulate the spirit of that dog).

His favourite cartoon was Spiderman, which was brave because he was scared of spiders and would always get someone else to do the jar thing whilst he cuddled his mother's skirt. His favourite food was beans on toast. He would awake when his alarm clock told him to, walk to school slightly late, and happily play with his best friends Martin Jenkins and Lucy Payne at break time. They were nice people who drifted away when the spots grew too frequent, but by then he had new groups of friends, armed as he was with a humour that belied his confidence.

For some reason, virtually all the world's population became a spider during the years after his childhood, and the jar-holders were too often girls with good hearts. They would do his nasty work for him, protect him, and then he would run to mother and offer them no gratitude for their effort. Not that he talked to his mother about any of that; his family were rarely communicative about anything as troublesome as trouble with relationships. Having learnt these lessons at home, he never really felt safe to talk to people about how he was scared of those girls in his late childhood, how they had wanted things from him that he didn't have, and didn't understand why they even asked.

Years later, his first sexual girlfriend was Moira Lindsay, a stupid girl whose unattractiveness made him slightly nauseous when she had her clothes on. It was a horrible first experience: overwhelmed as he was, he swore he would never do it again, which was when he first learned to separate his mental perception from his body. 'Children have it so easy', his teenage mind concluded, 'they want to play, they play; they want to eat, they eat. When you become an adult you want an awful lot of things you cannot have'. Freedom from the madness of his own sexual desire was one thing the teenage Carrick wanted to have but could not. He found it tormenting, embarrassing, and utterly bizarre not to be in control of his self, and to be increasingly told to find ways to be that which he simply could not be.

The only person to rescue Carrick from his own self-alienation was George. George was a handsome boy at school; he was caring, he was deep. He also had a touch that Carrick felt on many of his nights, until he awoke, disarmed, warm and repulsed at who he had become again.

So confused was he by these dreams that his visits to George's house were an adventure playground for his neuroses, and he drew up several behavioural rule lists which were completely arbitrary.

One of these rules was not to sit on George's bed – only the chair, just the chair – and this became de rigueur. He would go around George's house, sit on the chair, talk to him a bit about everything that meant anything to him, and then leave. "Phew. What was wrong with that?" he would say to himself, shutting the door with inner and outer exhalations: "I didn't even sit on the bed!"

The unfulfilled desire was what was wrong with that: the torturous, hungry maggot which gnaws its way to the centre of every being had pierced his skin. His suspected homosexuality then became segregated and denied, a whole other part of Carrick's personality now distorted from its original shape. His emotional world was fragmenting like a melting sheet of ice, its pieces drifting apart with slow yet unstoppable certainty.

He noticed of course, and wondered why, but with the final blow of his eventual George-less-ness due to an argument, he lost his ability to talk to the one person who both spoke and listened in his life. He stopped talking to other people and even stopped talking to himself. Instead, he ate his father's Shepherd's Pie, spent his mother's money and argued affectionately with his annoying sister. But the silence crept on like winter into his young heart: depression, suicide, ice.

It was a teenage winter, however, and the season soon changed. He stayed alive. Relationships came and went; he just couldn't cope with them. He hurt people tremendously and felt nothing, never explained why this was the case even though they pleaded with him to. He laughed at the care they had for him to their faces and then hid his insecurities behind a mask of sexual animalism and recognized the same in everyone and in everything he saw. Sometimes he was unsure which was hiding which, the animalism or the innocence, and what there was to be ashamed of.

He thought of his primal self with disgust at times, of the number of people he had slept with, and how he had lowered himself. At other times, he would feel an inexperience that would, he feared, destroy him should it be revealed and made open, and so he had to destroy this side of himself before it could have the chance to.

Eventually, he became so insistent on denying his desires that the child within him shrivelled and shed like a skin. Seeing only the human world, he subconsciously filtered every street and sky into categories of 'There' and 'Not There', and nature was alien, only the human world belonged. He walked down a street and could no longer see trees to be climbed, the daisies ripe for chaining, or feel the wind begging for kites. For he busied himself with the maelstrom of influences from the world around him: scattered, bedraggled signs pointing this way and that, but none of them inwards. His inside, however, was where everything communicated to Carrick that was true and relevant, and so Carrick became untrue and irrelevant to the only judge that counts: himself. He no longer cared who he was, what he said, the acts he was responsible for or the jobs that he took. He just was, and made sure he was not even that so far as he could.

Unfortunately, unbeknownst to his conscious self, Carrick's time was up. The hands of his life's clock had turned their final circle, and in planning a dull, savage slide into old age and pointless extinction, he had unwittingly wasted his final hour in a bored contemplation of nihilism and some obligations for wives and children which he could not bring himself to want and would not have to pretend to anyway.

One night in the autumn of his twenty-ninth year, as Carrick was driving home from work on a picturesque summer's day, he was aggressively introduced to the car that would kill him. There was not enough time between life and death to contemplate the journey, to bask in his successes and commiserate about his failures, to reminisce of childhood sweethearts un-kissed or to forgive and forget.

He simply died.

THREE

"My heart was gone by the time I died – I know that now. Yet when I felt myself have no heartbeat, it was one of the most terrifying experiences of my life. I was not at all drunk and I was doing nothing wrong, yet I couldn't stop it from happening. A man drove into the back of my car, and all of a sudden I was lying in the middle of the motorway, feeling my pulse slow and stop in my own veins. I cried out for my mother, for Beth.

"I felt the reassuring presence of angels, and light, and then one of the angel figures said that I should never ever worry again, and I was taken somewhere beautiful.

"There were angels or some kind of graceful figures moving towards an area with a huge floor. Everything was the colour turquoise. There were statues of honoured people as tall as skyscrapers. Yet to get to that place they asked me to pass through a checkpoint. Light wasn't running straight, and it was nothing like Earth in terms of skin and rock and solidity. There was some type of angel standing in front of me. He was made of light, emotion and perception, and I was looked through as if I were the same. It asked me, "What is your name?"

"It was a question which had deep importance and resonance, and the answer was definitely not 'Carrick'. I could not remember that name right then, but looking back now I understand that it was not the required answer. The name 'Carrick' had been a temporary, vulgar label. It was not the name I needed to remember. I was asked to say the name of my eternal self. I could not remember it and I was sent back here.

"When I awoke from the experience every inch of my body was in pain. I couldn't have imagined it was possible to feel such a sense of shock at what had happened. Now I am here, Doctor Turnstone, and this really happened. But you won't believe me, will you?"

"Thank you, Carrick. That was highly moving," Doctor Turnstone said, unemotionally. He reached over to his desk to get a piece of paper from another file. "We can talk more about this next time when I will tell you about research that has been done in the field of Near Death Experiences, so that hopefully we will find a way for you to re-adjust after having had such a traumatic experience."

"It wasn't only traumatic, Doctor," Carrick corrected him confusedly. "Oh, I know. Yet it also cannot have been incredibly relaxing for you to have had everything that you know challenged so dramatically and emphatically as you say. Am I correct in thinking you are angry that you were never informed about this place?"

"Yes, very angry indeed."

"I get the impression, then, that along with the happiness of having had the sensations you describe, you also hold resentment towards people and ideas which led you down other pathways than the one which leads to what you have felt and seen after dying."

"All pathways lead to the same place, I just need to see the path as I tread it to walk with sureness."

"But on a more specific point - for such quests as those of which you speak take a lifetime, if they are ever fulfilled at all – you must realise that the words you say affect others. Your sense now of having understood nothing prior to this experience of death, and that you had achieved nothing in life as you misunderstood its purpose, is a profound thing to say to people who care about you and who were probably there for you when you first had those experiences which you now dismiss so readily."

"I understand; I just can't seem to stop anymore."

"I would quietly advise you to try. Try to refrain from speaking about such things outside of this room until we have addressed them here, please?"

"But Doctor, how could I have achieved anything when I did not know why I was here?"

This angered the Doctor a little, for he was impatient, always wanting to have all the answers in no time, and he lost his temper, which was unlike him. "In some ways, you give the distinct impression that the experience has led you to conclude that this life is not right for you anymore—"

"No, it's not that—"

Carrick was interrupted.

"But you are missing the point: we all achieve something, Carrick, that is life. It is a matter of opinion though, Carrick, as to what one has achieved. Of course, we would all like to be Gandhi or Einstein or whomever, but we can't all be such people. The most important thing is to care for the people around you, to enjoy yourself, and to pursue those experiences which bring you happiness. When you are alienating people and will not see yourself for what you are – which is a perfectly normal and healthy young man who has had a very traumatic experience – you become detached from reality and others. You cannot see clearly what you are doing or the impact of your actions on people who care about you for who you are, not for who you would like to be. So please don't talk like this anymore outside of this room."

"Doctor Turnstone, I am not saying that I would like to be anything or anyone that I am not. On the contrary, I am saying that I was not who I really am beforehand, and that I would like to be who I am and not keep lying to everyone, which, yes, will perhaps make people happy for now but not in the long run. I do not have to be Einstein or Buddha or anyone else, because I am me. The only reason I speak of my life as I do is because I have seen the truth. I have, I swear it, Doctor. I have seen the truth and now all previous truth is redundant."

"Well, can you at least refrain from speaking about it until we have addressed the issue?"

"No."

Doctor Turnstone was angry. He had wanted to give an impression of 'immediate difference' to Carrick's family, who were paying him a lot of money to make him stop saying things that broke his mother's heart. Carrick had been a likeable young man up until his accident from what the Doctor had heard, but was seemingly determined to upset people these days. The Doctor was well-trained in the art of verbal restraint but his eyes spoke in sentences full of insults.

"I would advise you to re-think that, Mister Ares. See you next week."

FOUR

Carrick hated Doctor Turnstone. He had never been to a psychiatrist when he had lived in a dark world, feeling small and full of fear. But now that he was awake and alive and that same dark world glowed, apparently there was a problem. Sometimes he thought it was all he could do to try to heartily laugh at the soothing ironies of life in a medicinal way.

It was now seven months after his Near Death Experience and he was almost entirely healed from his wounds, which could be well-hidden under a nice shirt and tie. In every way he had been re-born – or born – depending on your perspective.

Carrick had had a problem with mental digestion prior to his accident. Unquestioningly he would translate his experience of the world about him into the way in which others had presented it. Now he engaged with the world but, disappointingly, he found as a result that he didn't actually want a relationship with any of the things he had done in the past. Almost everything seemed less crucial to him, from the films he once loved to the drinks he once craved to the people he thought friends to the dreams he bled dry.

Since that morning when Carrick awoke from surgery, the first and only point to his life as soon as he was able to wobble his lips again was to question what had happened to him. What a revelation, he thought! But what would stay with him more than even the sensation of speaking from his heart for the first time was the reaction of his closest friends and family. His childlike exclamations that he now knew the details of the heavenly afterlife were greeted with shrieked cries for assistance and an increase in his drug dosages. 'How confusing', he thought, when his veins were clean long enough to permit assessment with any clarity. 'This must be what it's like to be born,' he thought to himself, 'which makes me a conscious baby'.

He was right! He WAS a conscious baby! Oh, the pain the child felt when he re-learnt his life with awareness.

FIVE

Now, consider the book so far to be the conclusion to the last part of your life. Everything you have ever regretted can be forgotten. All the pain, humiliation, reckless wastefulness of the beauty that is within you and all around you: all is gone if you do one simple thing. Kindly switch off your past-receptors and realise you were wrong. Once more, kindly, SWITCH OFF ALL YOUR PAST-RECEPTORS AND REALISE YOU WERE WRONG!

No, it is not that simple, is it? For all of you, these words will simply be some more words and not an introduction at all.

There is an up-side to our habitual clinging to pasts, which is the assurance of people's company and empathy: most people hold the past far too close to their present, bringing pictures and letters and nicotine stains on their teeth with them everywhere they go. In going along with this idea, we hold the like-minded around us like stitches in a warm, woollen coat, in the winter of ignorance and distress currently engulfing the entire human race, with very few exceptions.

The warmth of the past provides reassurance of the existence of a future and reduces, therefore, the importance of the now. This warmth was no longer felt by Carrick, who had been inadvertently torn from the stitching by whoever had been driving the car which caused his life to end. That man seemingly had no such punishment, though, for physical punishment is so very different to the intangible suffering of desire. Did he experience revelations, or confusion of the kind which might end his life if he was not strong enough to deny its power? Carrick would wonder about such things.

Carrick had been stripped bare. This was an easy thing to sense both within him and without him and a much harder thing for him to convey in words; hard to discuss with oneself, hard to communicate to the outer world: 'I just don't understand you anymore'.

There had been a number of shifts in his sphere of acquaintance brought on by the upheaval of these events. For Carrick this meant his friends Peter and Stuart remaining close friends and his family remaining family members of one kind or another, whilst everyone else ran, or hid, or both.

Peter was Carrick's Sixth-Form friend, who lived on the same street as him and very seldom made a comment about anything, which was why Carrick's had previously got on so well with him. Stuart was a different type of person altogether. He broke the mould for Carrick's usual choice of friend. Stuart Randall had a brain, a heart and a spiritual side. The trouble was, at least two of these were pumped full of the most atrocious poison; they were full of rubbish! Carrick did not care for either of these people anymore, in truth. He also questioned seriously if he ever had. He looked at them carefully when they visited, and decided that although he had a new-found respect and love for all people, it did not mean he wanted to be around them. He did not care for the way Peter acted as if nothing had happened, and he did not care for Stuart telling him what had happened according to theories he had read in the books of strangers, without ever really having a clue how the experience had changed Carrick. Mostly though, Carrick just did not care.

He was fixated on how he could have ended up so blind in the first place. He would endure the sleeplessness of the adrift, of those who had lost their grip on life's meaning and purpose and were now floating in the grey areas between worlds of black and white, here and there, dead and, well, almost-dead. It was here which beings skulked who had lost their belief in what they are told is real and have found it to be a house that shares a garden fence with the entirely imagined.

The friends who ran from Carrick and his ideas would gossip about him among themselves. They would often talk of how they would hate to be as he was now, so changed, so different. They looked at each other over their biscuits or their beer, and all agreed, with whispers and wincing faces, that it must be a fate worse than death!

He didn't feel the sadness of the suicidal; it was much more serious. He felt the sorrow akin to those who had committed suicide, arrived in the after world and sensed somehow that they had made a mistake that would be impossible to rectify.

After a while he started to look as lost as the world as it twirled helplessly in space. His axis was tilted and, spinning, he became caught in the energetic fields of heavenly bodies that circled close by him but never touched.

SIX

"You know when you just care about someone so much that you feel you'd give your life for them if you could, just to show them?"

Carrick was present on the space-time continuum, but that presence was all he could contribute, and it was too much for him to attempt anything more. A single scheduled necessity occurred twice a week, though, in the form of the psychiatry of a Doctor Paul Timothy Turnstone.

"Oh, what a hard life you have!" the Doctor exclaimed, distractedly. No, he didn't fully understand. Having to listen to Carrick address yet another of his issues so near to his lunch break was also wearying the professional. But Carrick failed to notice, and instead reverted to an adolescent mode of communication, based on minimal interaction: mirroring, hiding, hoping no one would know and that everything would eventually be 'okay' in an hour or so. Although he felt in the right place within, he was so lonely and had no ability to realign his true self or express himself to a stranger at that time. Either the shape of the moment or the strength of their relationship had to change for this to be possible.

Even though the Doctor was showing very little understanding of whatever he might have processed from their interaction, Carrick's replies echoed each tone the Doctor set. If the Doctor made porridge of a serious point, Carrick would provide a wooden spoon.

"Yes, it's a positive marathon of pleasure," he joked.
"Pleasure?"

The psychiatrist was confused now, relieving Carrick of having to pretend to be otherwise. He had been coming to these sessions for nearly three weeks, and nothing had changed except for the way in which he now felt clinically rather than casually misunderstood. He had lost touch with his old self to such an extent that he sometimes felt he had forgotten how to be understood at all. Had forgotten how something as strange and unique as a human being can conceal their exceptional nature in a mirage of normality - the games one plays to deceive the outside world and its inhabitants, as well as (fingers crossed) oneself. Honestly, nakedly bewildered he stood these days – with excellent posture!

It was hard for the two of them to find any common ground. They had difficulties discussing the idea of a possible conversation about a conversation. What made matters worse was that - bafflingly, for someone paid as much as he was to do the intricate work he was doing - the Doctor had somehow perceived that Carrick's name was nothing but a front for his true identity as someone called James. The misnomer was applied repeatedly, and did not help an already strained relationship, but the Doctor seemed unable to help himself in this case. "Do please listen, James...sorry…sorry, Carrick!" he would say, laughing awkwardly, in an attempt to maintain the sense that this was still a regular mistake and not yet a habit. "Listen, Carrick, we need to start making some progress here. Can you help me?"

"If I can," the unimpressed Carrick volunteered, generously. "Thank you, Carrick" he said, emphasising his now pinpoint name-accuracy. "Please, let's go through things from the beginning. We'll make a list of what you've been through, what problems you face, and what we can do about them. Then, once we've accomplished that, I'm going to ask you to dust down your crystal ball, look into your future and start to find some things there which make sense to you and make you happy. Okay?" "Yes," said the patient optimistically. "Thank you." "So what we have so far is the life story of a successful young man, who has been through a highly traumatic experience...sorry." Carrick grimaced at the plain, black-and-white interpretation of what he had been through. However, the Doctor believed in nothing. He had no faith in heaven or hell or any life-after-death phenomena, and if someone claims to have experienced life beyond the physical then he or she has made a perceptual error that he would then explain. But he was making a meal of it so far! "Sorry, James," the Doctor continued as he put his hand on Carrick's knee in swift apology. "Carrick! Argh. Let me begin again! Sorry! Well, you were a very well and able man by all accounts until..." Carrick closed his eyes.

"What now?" snapped the Doctor at the sight of Carrick's voluntary blindness. "You're not listening to me", Carrick said wearily. "I've told you so many times. I wasn't happy."

"Well, who is happy, Carrick? I mean, this is a highly abstract term, very subjective in definition and really, how do you measure this against some kind of norm? I'm merely painting an objective picture, and happiness, however strong, is subjective, and therefore a different kettle of fish to the picture I'm trying to put together. I am only clarifying why we are here." Hand gestures concluded his point, whilst kettles of fish were gathered next to pictures of successful young men in Carrick's mocking mind's eye.

"Please may I continue?" the Doctor continued.

"We're here because I was unhappy."

"I beg your pardon?" exclaimed the Doctor, who was growing as impatient as his patient.

"I called the experience towards me."

"The experience of nearly dying?"

"Yes. I wasn't living, and I didn't know this, so I decided on some level to die and be born again in order to really live."

Another pause took centre stage in the conversation.

Doctor Turnstone had already come across ideas like Carrick's. He was a well-read man despite his conversational appearances, and theories like these had not escaped his attention. To him they were an expression of people's desperate attempts to explain why they were here, and why traumatising events have happened to them. The Doctor had tremendous sympathy for such people and saw this as a last resort of the human mind as it tried to come to terms with the horrors of life. It appeared to him the mental equivalent of the human body's protective habit of shutting down pain receptors in potentially fatal emergencies - except in this case the mind shuts down its intellectual sensors and accepts anything to numb the pain. "I haven't heard you talk like that before, Carrick. What have you been reading?"

Carrick wiped his moist forehead repeatedly. "Lots of things," he said obscurely.

"Like?"

"Anything."

His thoughts were dominated by a sense of loneliness which in turn affected his tongue and the room in quick succession.

The door was jammed when Carrick returned home. So he waited for Beth aimlessly in the local shop, reading the day's newspapers under the shopkeeper's judgemental gaze. His hands shook and his concentration was forced; he couldn't blame the shopkeeper for eyeing him the way he did. 'Still,' he thought, 'I could buy back some pride here,' and he bought something that he didn't even want to retrieve that which he so dearly did.

Beth and Carrick's relationship had been unstable since the accident. Carrick felt a whole new purpose in life; one that didn't involve her. All the little things she did grated on him in ways unfamiliar to his heart, and yet he was not alone in feeling love's season change, as Beth was making clearer to him with each day.

At first he had had the sympathy of those bound by blood or circumstances to love him; a knee-jerk reaction caused them to rally to his side in gratitude for his survival and care for his future. Yet within days of his waking, the humane call-to-arms had been muddled by Carrick's changed outlook. Corridor meetings ensued in which Carrick became the endless topic of discussion: "What did he say?", "He needs help.", "He's obviously been affected very badly".

It began to seem that Carrick had gone insane. He talked of souls more than television, and never seemed really engaged with the serious task of making his way back to work and social life. Worst of all, he had started making statements about people that were horrifyingly true.

Face after face would drop at his side, having entered the room as a picture of grace and concern. "You need to eat more," he told his self-conscious cousin, Sarah, as she refused another grape, "self-loathing isn't beautiful." "Are you pretending to be happy for my sake, Aunt Mary? If so, please stop because it's making me sad." "Are you speaking from your heart when you say that, Simone, because it sounds like something you just read in the paper." It never ended.

There was no filter anymore, or care for one, and it became impossible to sit for even an hour with Carrick without feeling as if you were made of glass and confusion. Nobody dared risk it after a week: they would rather sit at home either pondering his words or trying not to.

When he got out of the hospital he was told that part of the recovery process involved psychiatric check-ups, but the way in which he was informed – by his parents and girlfriend and not the hospital – left Carrick in no doubt as to whose needs were being catered for, although he said nothing to them at the time. His mother stared endlessly at the floor.

At his first session with the Doctor, Carrick became nervous and was therefore misunderstood. But being told you are wrong to feel what you have never felt to be so true is not a pleasant experience for anyone, and under the weight of so-called professional interpretation, Carrick felt borne down upon by the meeting's end. He returned from it to argue ferociously with the person he was most needing to be close to. Beth's opening statement only stoked the fire - she was asking for it – as she explained, without adequate preliminaries and politeness, how uncomfortable he had made people and why 'seeing someone' was necessary in her eyes.

"You've changed, Carrick!"

"Thank God!" he exclaimed. "I was a corpse before. Don't tell me you loved him more than me. Why aren't you happy for me? I'm happy."

Beth wasn't, and Carrick had lain awake every night since the conversation, feeling himself in a strange new world without help. He knew Beth was not asleep because he could feel her presence there beside him. Still he did nothing to reach for her. For hours they stayed like that, and dawn separated them again.

Standing in the newsagent's that day the door was jammed, he finally got the call he was waiting for, and it was her. She spoke to say that he should return. He approached the light of their home together with the warm glow of joy one feels before stepping inside their door on a cold winter's night. He turned the key but the door remained unmoved, so he knocked until a familiar face answered, and then he kissed it.

"This door is awful. The lock must have got stiff from the cold because it won't open anymore," he informed her, innocently.

"No, it will," she replied, and the truth dawned on him.

The next day, Carrick told Doctor Turnstone how he felt about the end of his relationship. He remembered the small details which torment at the conclusion of such intimacy, the things which are embarrassing to speak of. He crumbled when thinking of them.

Carrick's desperation melted his previous solidity, and this time the tangible subject matter was accessible to the doctor. At last it had happened: Carrick had revealed his weakness and the doctor could show his strength. It was the real beginning of their relationship. Soon, they would sail amid great seas of thought, and have a new land in sight.

SEVEN

The Doctor, with his scientific knowledge and practical stance soon emerged as the perfect sparring partner for Carrick. 'James', whoever he was, was not heard of again. A dynamic became established between them, with the Doctor arguing for science and Carrick probing into spirituality. In no time their sessions grew enraging and hysterical, passionate but thoughtful, and they enjoyed them once they felt safe in each other's company.

"What's a flower?"

"Don't be stupid, Carrick! I think we know what a flower is."

"What would you describe a flower as being?"

"A stem, with some petals, a bud, a pollen holder, that kind of thing…" the Doctor returned.

"Yes, a human being."

"No, a flower." He was annoyed, but Carrick would go on, and on, on and on…

"Any human being is exactly like this. Petals – physical adornments, buds – genitals, leaves – hair to guide the rain off us. There's only one exception: a mind. If a flower could think, what would it do?"

The Doctor thought for a moment. "It would probably hold on to its pollen, and see the bees as a threat." He seemed proud of his answer.

"Exactly! And that's the human way of seeing things – that to hold on to what makes life will make it better. But the flowers would soon die if they thought such things. The pollen of a human is its love, its gifts. But the way a lot of people think is that they must keep it all in, having been taught that if we give them away we somehow lose something, or must ask for a price in return."

"So what are you saying? What's your point?"

"That if we didn't have minds life would be better."

"I think you are in the wrong place!" the Doctor laughed. As did Carrick; he then carried on with a sense of seriousness.

"Had they minds, most things about flowers would change and not necessarily for the better. But we worship minds as the be-all-and-end-all, the one thing we have which 'separates' us from nature and makes us evolved. Actually, it's really clear that our minds are harming us. There are so many ways of thinking about things that our minds are nothing but tornadoes, crushing our experiences like storms. We can't just be anymore because people have to do whatever they are told they should be doing. I mean, my question is, don't you believe that if the wind could think, or flowers, or anything like that, they would then be broken or changed? That they wouldn't be able to just 'be' anymore, in their natural beauty and perfection and efficiency because – especially if they had the ability to communicate their thoughts – other flowers or things would start telling them what to do and how to be, and that because they work already, it could only end in disaster."

Doctor Turnstone thought about it seriously. "I'm not entirely sure I know the answer to this question."

"Please speculate."

"I see your point. And it's very good. I have spent many years of my life studying nature in the form of our knowledge of physics, chemistry, biology and all kinds of other things. It's a fascinating, interconnected, and in many ways flawless system. And yes, humans are doing an awful job of being part of it and appreciating its needs, respecting the little consideration it needs to function. It's quite astonishing that all it needs is to be allowed to be, and we can't even seem to be able to let that happen."

"Yes!"

Carrick was ecstatic. "That's exactly what I'm saying! That we're not allowing ourselves to be – that we too are natural and we too must be left to be and as a result will function well. But we keep messing with the formula, and it's like we're trying to destroy ourselves in consequence, because we won't let our nature rule us as it naturally does."

"Would you like to have no mind?"

"I can see that it harms us in some ways, when we consider it the most important thing in our world."

"But how would we know what to do if we could not think?"

"What do you mean 'to do'?"

"To do! Action is life and energy in constant motion – we can never just be and not do, it is technically impossible. To have a mind to express our talents and be aware of our actions beyond merely existing is a beautiful thing! We are not only numbly at the mercy of all nature; we can change our external world according to our thoughts."

"That is why thoughts are so dangerous. If we had clearly moulded thinking, then this argument would be valid, but there are no thoughts we have made that can overcome the natural wonder that is within us and around us. Therefore we create disorder inside, with aims and goals which change and are always unclear, both inside ourselves and in the mass world around us!"

"But to have no direction, would you like that? What achievements would you gain?"

"You would not value or conceive of achievements, because they are based on the idea that something is missing and you need to do or obtain something to complete yourself, or that you can be somewhere much better than where you are now. Without that thought, you would only do things because you felt you wanted to, not with the idea of getting something you don't have now. That idea portrays people as full of holes, and tries to fill them with things, but people are complete and beautiful just living as they see fit. Only they're not thinking that way."

"But not all people are superstars or whoever they want to be in their wildest dreams!"

"There you go! There you go – that's exactly it. Why have you just said that? The whole picture which that creates is that I am somehow incomplete now, as opposed to how I would be, were I a superstar. This is a mental idea of the world. It has been produced because in a money-driven, success-driven state of mind people feel they have to try harder, be more, because unless they are the best they haven't got to where they want to go. It is funny no one notices how often even superstars self-destruct and go down in a sinking ship of self-loathing and depression, while young mothers can be as happy as beans just running around with their new-born."

"I'm just saying that it's common to want to be big and successful. It's not that there is only one definition of this, though, you're right in that, and I have to unpick this many times in my line of work because the effect these thoughts have on general well-being is catastrophic. But if you have achieved something monumental, oftentimes it is because our minds and feelings have interacted and we are overjoyed at what the mind has created."

"But is this really the case? Do we really feel this way? We are told we do, but in my personal experience many of the things I have achieved caused me the worst moments of my life - feelings of emptiness and a hollow idea of what life is about. I have no need for them, place no value on them. I don't even know where they came from; I don't think they were mine.

"I mean, with the education process you are subliminally implanted with this idea that if you were left to grow alone in the world, you wouldn't know it or know what to do with it. It is as if we are told that we are fools who must learn, empty batteries which need charging with power. But that's not true. We are *not* ignorant and powerless upon birth; on the contrary we are all filled with ideas and the strength to use them, and should be given what we need to fulfil our natural desires, and this is why people get so upset. They try so hard at what they are told is progress whilst the only thing they actually achieve is to lose touch with themselves and feel empty or incomplete. Will that make people happy, having their natural desires usurped by other people?"

"But if you get good grades at school, and are able to do a job you can be proud of, you can earn more money for your effort and buy the things you need."

"But they have all been confiscated! They are free by natural law, but have been confiscated by the rich and put behind bars, and money releases them."

"That seems fair to me. Why should anything that has taken time and money to make be given away for free?"

"Well, yes, but the people who made those things are usually the very ones that the bars are designed to keep out." There was a silence.

"Now is that fair?"

There were more silences as a sticking point was in their midst now: it is unfair. It is. Still, the inevitable rejoinder was made by the doctor.

"Well, they could earn more money if they increased their skills."

"How many skills does the Queen have? How much time does a working class person have to dedicate to learning when she or he is working so much that they are nothing except tired in the little remaining time? Not to mention people all over the world, working in dangerous conditions to fuel the endless 'doing' and 'achievement' and 'production'."

"I don't really see where all this is going, Carrick. We are not here for a philosophy class."

"What I'm saying is, I'm looking back over my life, and I can't believe what I see there."

"What do you see?"

"Someone who never once used their feelings to guide them, but always thoughts, and not even their own, just what they heard or picked up off someone else. I have a mind, Doctor, but I don't know what it has been doing up until now? You ask me to write down things I want to achieve from now on, some kind of future that would make my life worthwhile, and I can't see anything. And the point is this, what is not worthwhile about just being?"

"It is not sustainable. You need money and things to eat and live."

"But there are trees and fields and they are said to belong to people – I am not allowed to touch them as they are not mine. I could eat and live naturally, but instead I must adhere to aims that are not mine and give my time to things I don't want to do, in order to get what naturally is mine to take."

"But you must like the blessings of the modern, developed world: you can't live with just straw and mud and berries!"

"But I can't live on ignorance and brutality and slavery either. Some are being paid and treated more fairly than others but there is a pattern to how, in being nourished physically, we are impoverished in every other form of existence. You asked me to think of aims, Doctor, but I have no aims. I don't want to work anymore."

"How will you live?"

"I don't know – which makes me not want to live at all…" the Doctor looked worried, "and that's not natural. So you see, from the natural child wanting merely to play and love and eat and survive, we are becoming something grotesque. It's called evolving, but it's a stripping away of all our nature, and a manipulation of all that we are. So I'm saying that if you take away nature, instead of evolving to some higher plane, we descend into depression and feelings of worthlessness, desiring only not to be here or do this anymore. We are slaves, with material adornments instead of whiplash scars."

"So you have no idea what you are here for anymore, don't want to achieve anything, and are becoming suicidal?"

"No. I know why I'm here. I know what I want to do. And I want more than anything to do it. But it is being taken away from me."

"What is it you want?"

"Nothing: to be free to be whatever I would like to be. To not know a plan, and so always be at peace knowing that I will never fail with nothing to achieve but living the best I can moment to moment, according to standards I have set and not anyone else. It's like the carrot on the string tied above the donkey's head: this idea that there's success waiting out there for us only works if the donkey is stupid enough not to figure out that there is grass beneath its feet but that the carrot is never coming to them; otherwise it would just graze."

"That's very negative, Carrick. No one's making donkeys out of anyone really, are they? There is a structure in which you can be whatever you would like to be. You can get more than what you would achieve on your own, you just must sacrifice some of your time and use your talents and make some effort to get those things."

"In theory, that's what it is, and yes, that's what we're told to believe it is. But it's turned into a process in which you sacrifice everything you are to get what you don't even want, but what you have been made to feel you need by the insecurities that advertising and marketing implant in you. The whole thing stinks. The whole infrastructure of the world as I live and breathe it is designed to take away all my power and make me feel arrogant or evil for wanting it back. This is not a life. This is a slow, torturous death, satiated by bursts of what we actually want in the form of sex, love and food."

Silence opened the wound of the words in a Doctor who believed in the way of life Carrick had mercilessly chucked aside, who had worked hard to achieve the things Carrick said were worthless, who felt his whole desire to help people was aided by the systems within which he had moved, and that he was a higher, happier, more able human being as a result of adhering to them.

"Carrick, do you think I'm wasting my life?"

Carrick had been so wrapped up in his own world that he had forgotten who he was talking to; his enemy personified. He had blown all his secrets and all his battle plans lay open on the table, yet with the other side wounded and the mission complete, he felt only the sadness of his foe. Peace was all he had wanted anyway. 'Why do we have to fight and disagree?' he thought. 'Why can't the doctor have his way of life and I, mine? That is the question.'

"Sorry. I can see I have insulted and upset you. If what you do makes you happy, that's what I believe you should do. But I can't do what I want to do, so I become enraged so often these days. I guess neither way is right or wrong, it's just what you want to do, or yes, achieve. I want to achieve nothing but peace in myself. I've been scarred and bruised, Doctor. I've been through a lot, and you're right, it has affected me. I lie awake at nights, I can't sleep and I can't eat. I can't remember what joy feels like sometimes and I don't know why I'm here or what I should do in terms of fitting into the outside world. I can't relate to anyone and wherever I go I see hardship. There's no joy for me because I want the joy of freedom. And people tell me I am wrong so I have fought for it in my head, fought for my right to do what I want to do, but have found nothing, no right to do what I want to do. I do owe everything in my life to others, and am frustrated at my own uselessness and inability to reciprocate. Since my experience of life beyond here, Doctor, I have become a taker, and all I have is my head to help me hide from this. I guess my aim is to hide and to think and to justify my hiding and my thinking as something worthwhile. I am not free of aims at all. This is my aim: to find shelter from the storm... I'm sorry."

The Doctor called an end to the session and it left him troubled for some time. When he met with other patients he would now wonder what their aims in life were, wondering if Carrick was right and that he and everyone else was being fed the idea of what they wanted to do or be. He felt his deepest concept of self as it asked his surface ego questions that he would never usually think about. The natural state of man, free from all artifice, seemed a caveman to him yesterday, but today something wondrous.

EIGHT

"Carrick?"

"Yes?"

"There was something you asked me which I have been thinking about a great deal. It was phrased something like this: had I loved someone enough to die for them in the name of love, to prove how much I cared for this person?"

"Yes, I remember. You didn't answer."

"I know, and I feel sorry for this; I was listening." The Doctor rustled his papers. "I've felt a strong need to answer that question since we last met."

"Please, go ahead."

"Being a married man, I have never once felt the need to demonstrate my love for my wife, or anyone else for that matter, with behaviour that is self-destructive. It strikes me as something profoundly missing the point it is trying to make, for destroying one's self is surely not an act of love, in any sense of the word."

Carrick nodded.

"Well, I had three questions which I now want to put to you, if you would be so kind as to answer them. My first question is: what would be the point of giving your life for someone who presumably loves you, too? After this, my second question would be: why would a person even ask this? And finally, I would like to know how you think she or he would benefit?"

"What a stupid set of questions – have you ever thought *about anyone* besides yourself? What were they again?"

"I've forgotten!" the Doctor joked.

The bitterness of Carrick's words had seemed sweet to him at the time. The doctor thought for a while. "Well, first, what is the point of sacrificing one's self for another that supposedly cares for them?"

Carrick considered this for the briefest amount of time.

"To show who you value; it is normal to put ourselves before all others, so to make a statement of the opposite is a sign of who means the most to you."

"Okay", the Doctor disagreed, "let me hold on to this thought, but it brings me to my second question of why they would ask someone for such a demonstration of their care."

"Perhaps it is not them asking," Carrick immediately responded.

"Ah-ha! So it is latent within the person themselves, this self-destruction, and love is merely providing an excuse for it to be manifested as something more positive. Well, that is, if you are saying what I think you are saying, it is they who are asking this of themselves."

"What does 'latent' mean?"

The doctor looked puzzled. "Hmm, latent," he repeated, as if it could possibly be a self-defining term... It was at this point when, facing the window and the greyness of life outside the room, he understood something about one of the people who coloured it from within. What rose up in his understanding was a wider point about life, that every entity requires something other than itself in order to define what it is.

The presentiment that then crept over the Doctor was that perhaps Carrick was not all he seemed - what lurked beneath the surface of this outwardly courageous, self-sacrificing person? Carrick was perhaps even self-destructive, and looking for another to activate this within him, and then to displace it onto them, calling it something about what it is to love.

"Latent: adverb," he read, "hidden, concealed; existing but not developing or manifest; dormant."

"No, I don't think that's true," Carrick decided after considering the idea. "And, no, in fact, I wasn't implying that it was me who saw self-sacrifice as a wonderful thing – as if!"

The doctor immediately readjusted his interpretations, and continued upon his mission to dissect the thing more penetratingly.

"What were you alluding to then, pray?"

"'Pray': an interesting choice of words; I was actually getting to this exact point. It's a very religious idea, to love; the highest idea of love is not that of human to human, but of the human to the divine, to God or whatever term is prevalent at the time and place concerned."

"You have been thinking about this a lot?"

"Yes! A lot!" Carrick laughed.

"Why?"

"Because it affects me all the time, all the time."

"What's that?"

"This idea of interaction; the structure it takes on as you live. It is distorted, and I can see how."

This was a rather arrogant statement for the Doctor's communicative tastes, but he wanted to understand how it had come to be spoken.

"What is the connection between ideas of piety, ideas of communication and ideas of love?" he asked bluntly.

"We fear God and love, and subordinate ourselves to them, which is a thought. It is a thought with more complex parts, but this is the central idea that causes one to believe that self-sacrifice is affectionate."

"So, the third query, as to how the object of love could possibly benefit from the sacrifice, what is the answer to this, if there is one at all?"

"There isn't one: God, if there is such a thing, whatever He or She or It is called, does not benefit from self-sacrifice, nor do lovers or friends or our good selves. I think it is a crucial misunderstanding of the human race, that hurting one's self is admirable and required if we are to prove the validity of what we feel towards another. And this is what I think about a lot these days.

"But the thought is persistently overpowering when it comes to our natural survival mechanisms. It is funny then, that piety and love of God – the most extreme form or elevated notion of what love can be – also often demand a sense of self-hatred and obedience. Who benefits from this? Is it the holy people who are the messengers of another world? Or governing bodies which keep power as a result of others' obedience and, as you say, ideas encouraging them to believe that they are not running their own lives? Who benefits?"

Carrick was asking the questions now, but the doctor had no answers. He understood that this was a very complex point; three questions alone could open its depths. Complexities such as this had no answers in dictionaries, and could not be resolved by the simple-minded associations of psychoanalytical metaphors or behavioural observation. Carrick had addressed an open-ended problem for the human race, and although the Doctor could identify it as important, he was not the person to help; he was not a healer of that kind or calibre.

NINE

Carrick Ares was a name which the doctor associated with many things pleasurable at that point in time: it conjured images of gladiators in Rome, dancers in a fire, of two beasts' eyes shining in pitch black – they were looking at one another, that was for sure. Doctor Turnstone was experiencing psychiatry as he had always imagined it could be; he had always longed for this. The conversations with his patient had been captivating, and the potential to help someone in such a dramatically bad shape was awakening, enticing. It reached through to him.

Whatever he had really seen, there were two things Carrick now valued as life's gifts and meaning: love and knowledge. Everything else had paled into insignificance for him, for he had never experienced love like he had when he died, and never wanted to know about life until after he had left it. It sickened him to think of what his instincts had become beforehand: he had used love and knowledge only to get what he wanted, which he had believed to be power.

Naturally, he now wanted to find out why and how this had happened. This was, after all, his life, something of value, not just something to get through any more. He looked at everything he could find to get explanations for how he had come to believe what he had believed and be who he had been. What had happened to his mind, and what was really going on in this thing called his life? He was fascinated by history, religion, nature, political ideologies: all those areas which make up The Rules and therefore the basis for all our understandings of this world. Yet something strange happened to him as soon as he looked at these notions and their makers: he began to realize how clear it is that there were never any 'rules' at all.

It would take just a few pages of reading in any history book for this to become obvious. The perception of human's identities and their universal environment self-evidently changes over time: it has never been the same between any two regions or at any two points in history. Setting aside his own previous conception of what history might be as much as he could, it seemed to him clearly that the only criterion was 'whoever shouts loudest' in proclaiming their ideas will make history, and decide who will lie in unmarked graves. He heard the voices of Roman emperors, war heroes, philosophers and prophets. He rarely heard the voice of a woman though, and almost never the voice of a peacemaker.

Besides those immortal figures who required no privilege of birth or exercise of violence to be heard eternally the rest of humanity's key figures seemed essentially monkeys: alpha males, banging their chests and screeching petulantly their vision-less claims to thrones or crowns and using fear and threats to repel their opposition. It was little wonder that by having humanity's definition and purpose in life predominantly shaped by violent, power-hungry men, the results are predominantly violent, power-led and male-centric, Carrick concluded.

Although it was at times utterly depressing and tiresome to turn the pages between one violent male and another, world history became fascinating to Carrick as it had never been before. He looked at all the areas of understanding, all the telescopes and kaleidoscopes through which people viewed their lives, and began to see exactly why his vision of life had been so blurred before. He had thought he was just merely here and living 'normally'. Now he understood that he had been recycling all the history the world had lived through while claiming these ways of life to be not only standard, but his own. He began to understand how he, like everyone else, was who he was because of what he had heard and seen and experienced. This began to develop within him a sense of compassion towards himself and others which as far as he could tell no one else had.

In terms of getting closer to the truth he sought, however, he was not much wiser. It was as if, up until his death, he had been merely a drop of paint on a canvas which, after a rather graceless trip across the studio floor, had become able to glance back at the picture of which he was previously only a small part. And in terms of what he had seen in that glance, he found to his immense dismay that there was simply no vision a mortal mind had conjured thus far which had either captured or explained it. Even with the kind of intense research he had previously avoided at all costs, the ideas people had created about who they are and what is going on were just too narrow, too closed-minded, too vain, too obsessed with their own agendas. Perspectives from a single standpoint, that's what they were, but not an image of the whole.

According to the books Carrick had begun to read so earnestly, the earliest anthropological evidence of religious thinking was intertwined with perceptions of nature. People noticed that the weather changed, and with it their hunting seasons or harvests and living conditions. They began to develop rain and sun deities. The first idea of a single God came from an Egyptian Pharaoh, Akhenaton, who saw god – or Aten, as he called him – as the sun.

It was so understandable, and highly logical. Nature was the deciding factor in most of human life for hundreds of thousands of years – before technology allowed society to move beyond the constrictions of seasonal boundaries. The elements would have seemed much more powerful in earlier eras of humanity than they did to a child-of-the-modern-world like Carrick, with his electric lighting to out-shine winter nights, his concrete home to withstand the winds and snow, and a technology which brought faraway places and peoples to his bedroom.

Technology gives the impression that humanity is overcoming nature, rather than working within it. But this questionable sense is extremely recent. It was not the case when the predominantly very old belief systems were developing. The idea that the divine was entwined with the forces of nature was an obvious conclusion from a grounded perspective. People did not know that the earth was a spherical planet at that time, could not see beyond their eye-line – where did the 'sun' go to, or the 'clouds' come from? There was no awareness of water cycles or photosynthesis or seasons in terms of movements in space and the axis tilt of the globe. The rain and sun must have seemed to come and go from somewhere or someone else.

Carrick could understand how the feeling of being helpless against nature might have affected the ideologies of early cultures. Looking up at a vast night sky, with twinkles of light evoking the size of an unimaginable realm, the early human beings would have reasonably deduced that the persons to their left and right were not its makers. Searching for answers, ideas would begin to circulate as to whom or what might be the creator.

It was a very mortal notion: that there had to be someone responsible. In the brief space of time humans live for, it was obvious that if things changed, it was because someone or something had caused it to. It was the logical basis for people to understand their own existence, and a natural conclusion to make given the state of their knowledge.

This process of interpreting the world through the five senses resulted in two of the most influential ideas in history. They are ideas which have since shaped everything human beings have thought about life and the way they have lived. The first was the notion of some realm or entity which was separate from the world. The second was the consequent reduction in humans' perceptions of their own autonomous power over the world and themselves. People began to feel they were living at the mercy of various forces that they could not see or touch or feel, let alone understand or be. This was a world which was only secondary to a much more important realm: one where all the decisions are made and powerful beings lived.

Very logical, very sensible, given the state of awareness at the time, but these perceptions were later portrayed not as imaginative interpretations appropriate to their time, but as facts. Long after humans have had the technology and knowledge to investigate life in more objective ways, many still deny this evidence and refer back to our primitive speculations as more reliable sources of information.

This would be tolerable, merely a quirk of the human experience, were the repercussions for all concerned not so utterly and constantly devastating. By deeming humanity's projected ideas to be absolute truth, some have got stuck on the first ones. The human race's ideas must develop in tandem with the human race's ability to understand the universe.

And so humanity's philosophical development continues to be somewhat illogical and slow. It explained to Carrick so well why people were still arguing over every single principle of belief systems and why many have become so confused by the whole thing that they have simply abandoned believing in anything. Every new insight takes a vast amount of time and struggle to be assimilated into mass culture, for it must become so blindingly obvious that there is not a single iota of possibility that it can be explained away using previous ideas.

An infamous and highly traumatic example of humanity's reluctance to evolve in terms of behaviour and belief was when the Hungarian physician, Ignaz Semmelweis, suggested in 1847, while working in Vienna General Hospital, that doctors wash their hands with chlorine before treating sick patients. Despite numerous reports that hand washing reduced mortality to below 1% in wards where the rate usually varied from 10%-35%, his theory was mocked and discredited in the medical community for much of his life.

As with the famous example of Galileo, imprisoned by the Catholic Church for insisting that the earth travelled round the sun, and not the other way round as some perceived it, Semmelweis went from being a man with a brilliant mind and future to one who bore the burden of trying to change peoples' perceptions. With his lone voice against a medical profession which destroyed the reputation of his findings, he began to suffer from anxiety disorders, and was reputed to abuse alcohol and indulge in prostitutes. Self-hatred and self-destruction is in evidence in such behaviour. This was understandable to some, given the alienation of his mind and spirit.

His theories rejected in spite of sound evidence, Semmelweis went on to spend much of his time and energies raging against the medical mainstream as irresponsible murderers and fools, until finally at the age of forty-seven he was lured into a mental asylum where he was beaten, straight-jacketed and confined to a dark cell. He died within two weeks, with severe internal injuries and gangrene poisoning from an infected wound, presumed to be a result of the beating he received on his arrival. Years after, the work of German physician, Robert Koch, reinforced the germ theory of the renowned French chemist and microbiologist Louis Pasteur, which suggested that disease was not spontaneously generated, as was the understanding of the time, but was caused by micro-organisms. This led to the findings of Semmelweis being proved correct.

The people who try to move humanity away from its original beliefs often suffer; they are killed and shamed and embarrassed until they either confess their mistakes, so that their adversaries may sleep soundly again with all questions remaining fully answered, or are made to appear to be lying or mad. Humans are thereby reassured that the whole truth was already found years ago.

Our pre-existing ideas about life are untouchable; they are ranked higher than our experiences, and when someone suggests that their own personal experience might contradict the ideas they have been given, they are in serious trouble. For they must speak against the crowd, who have been taught to fear change and being isolated from one another outside the group mentality, and so their only option – if they wish to spare themselves the terrible consequences of speaking openly of their novel experiences – is to disengage from their own senses. And Carrick realised that this was at the root of thoughts being placed above feelings.

TEN

There was something about the concept of thoughts being placed above feelings which Carrick could relate to completely. His experience of the truth in the afterlife had shown him that emotion, memories and the energies they produce and emit are really all there is. He saw that the way we dislike feelings and attempt to kill or betray them, and do what we think we should do instead of what we feel we should do, was one reason why he had lost himself so badly before his death.

In the time in which he was living, thinking was the way all 'evolved', 'civilised' and 'clever' people functioned; they did not feel if they could manage to avoid doing so. Feelings were embarrassing and uncontrollable. They were the shameful animal side of life which humans tried to pretend was not within them. Some said that feelings were just a mistake or a test of self-control which sorted the 'animals' from the highly evolved. At a time when control, power and all things technologically proficient were seen as desirable for the human state, feelings were put aside, if not voluntarily, then with great violence and distress by those whose emotions were free and strong enough to resist control by the mind alone. It was these people for whom anxiety disorders were a problem, and depression, and rage: society would then declare that these people themselves were the problem, or had been suffering from problems. The truth is that their life force had been powerful enough to not betray itself – too loyal to the cause of freedom to bear the uniforms of dispassion or death.

How ironic it was, after seeing how important feelings are in the afterlife, when Carrick realised that had he made a list of priorities in life before he died, he would not even have imagined feelings playing a part in it. Now he lived by feelings – he was genuinely moved to learn about himself in a way that he had never been by what he had been told would interest him. He started to neglect his friends and relatives, simply sitting with his feelings, as if they were able to take the place of all others. He found sometimes, oftentimes nowadays, that he did not want or need anyone except himself, and that he was on a pathway going inwards with beautiful scenery. The destination tantalized him with what it would feel like to be totally yourself; totally and utterly absorbed in one's own majestic, eternal being, never letting anyone tell you it was not real. He was his own drug of choice these days, and the adrenaline and hallucinations were beyond those he had known with any other.

Looking at the hatred of change which resulted after insisting our ideas about reality be considered absolute fact, it was not just the inevitable snail's-pace effect this had placed on humanity's development which was dangerous. The idea that we were helpless and at the mercy of creators and shapers of the world who are somehow not here, and not visible, provided a fantastic bed upon which people could lay all of their fantasies. Ironically it helped some to control others in a world where the most powerful species which inhabits the planet believes itself to have little power over either itself or its environment.

Following the concept of separate worlds and reduced human power, there came another phase in the evolution of our way of seeing life, which was the development of ideas about the characteristics of these separate realms – where they were, what was there, who was there, and what our relationship to them might be.

Carrick had read many atheist-penned books detailing the 'delusions' and 'manifestations' of the human imagination which, so these writers raged, have been permitted to run amok over all sense and logic since the situation had developed – of believing in things that could not be seen or touched, so long as they seemed to make sense. It upset him to dismiss people's entire worlds of thinking so easily and un-empathetically. After all, as Carrick knew now, there was very much more than this world alone.

Yet there could be no doubt that anyone looking to prove there is no God has plentiful evidence to support that claim. The obvious first point: it is not a physical being in the same sense as a man or woman. How one might meet the creator of life is impossible to comprehend and therefore it is hard to say that there is just one single entity responsible for it. No one could calm all doubters in this way. The second point, atheism's disgust with the extent to which belief in the intangible has been allowed to govern human being's understanding of life, is equally inarguable. If there were another realm with a divine being or beings, their question to the religiously faithful would be, 'why would this have happened? The message appears to have been subjected to an excessively mischievous game of Chinese whispers.

To consider in more detail the argument that deities are a human-made concept as opposed to humanity being created by a deity, it is interesting to observe the changes of beliefs regarding religion through the world's history. For example, originally, because ideas were so closely entwined with nature, divinity was a place of nature and creation. In some religions, aside from the sun gods and nature-controlling deities of early societies, the governing deity had a female face, because creation was associated with the birthing mother as the source of life, and so the creator of the Universe was considered female.

Carrick watched through the history books as matriarchal societies in Africa, and nature-loving pagan and Egyptian societies created and worshipped goddesses such as Isis and Brigit. But as large-scale war became more prominent, particularly around the time that led to the Roman Empire, the purpose of human life changed from survival, and living in nature's strong palm praying it would not close, to establishing and maintaining territory and setting up empires. Ideas about divinity underwent a transition to accompany the change, and the external presence became more commonly a male entity with masculine characteristics.

In the modern world, Carrick saw beliefs about life's governing external forces changing once more – in the technological age, as machines become more and more a part of everyday life, there would develop an increasingly powerful theology in the west in particular which perceived that, like machines, we humans simply produce, maintain ourselves and then die. Furthermore, like machines, people are told that what they want is power. This seemed to demonstrate yet further the non-believer's argument that our beliefs stem from us rather than revelation.

Carrick fed all this into his observation of how he had viewed love and knowledge before, and his quest for answers was not proving futile. So it made sense why he had wanted power, and had sought to employ love and knowledge and all his other skills as a means of getting power: it was the age he was living in. It was just another example of people having their ideas of life echo their ways of living, being unable to see beyond themselves. We have seen ourselves as peaceful creators and nurturers, as war-like peoples who conquer and kill, and now increasingly as machines that run on power.

We have been living through an immense period of male-god worship, however: from their inception to the twentieth century, all over the world, various very male gods of war and intolerance reigned. From The Crusades to the conquering of the Americas, the warriors and fighters were claiming to have one male deity or another firmly on their side. The inevitable, and repulsive, culmination of this phase of humanity was the world wars. In close succession Carrick read the gruesome stories of the two largest, most destructive organised acts of aggression in human history in the safety and disinfection of black and white. He read the combined number of deaths, seventy million people, and was unable fully to grasp the actuality of that many people losing their worlds to such futile slaughter. People began to see what the war mentality led to. Thus, the first generation to be born in the western world after these two great wars was the generation that reached adulthood in the 1960s.

Carrick read how this cataclysmic era produced a massive generational move away from war-like ideas and, not surprisingly, towards an outburst of violent desire for peace and love. There was a solid divide between the old and the new ways of thinking, signalled by the ageism of the younger generation – 'Don't trust anyone over 30' was a phrase coined at the time.

This post-war generation was naturally sick of war, and the beliefs which lead to war in previous generations' thinking. Instead they propelled messages of love: all you need is love, summer of love, free love, flower-power, peace-marching, make-love-not-war, legendary hippie-dom. Yet the disparity between war and peace mentalities was so sudden, and the remaining generation still so present, that it scared the existing people in power, and was not successful in creating the extreme change to social, cultural and religious practices that the people pressing for it seemed to desire. The murder of the public figures not adhering to tradition – John Lennon, Malcolm X, Martin Luther King and others within a few years of each other – bore witness to this. Such figures were from all areas of society – once again new ideas challenging the old were rejected and extinguished using whatever means necessary to resist the potential for changes to our ways of thinking. The freedom that was created by this era profoundly altered everything that went after. It saw a back-lash against hippies and radical thinkers, a resurgence of conservative ideas, yet the sixties have also led to ways of living which are more peace-embracing. It has brought about ways of life without the degree of prejudice faced by many people previously.

Carrick himself had existed almost completely in the shadow of the 1960s all his life, drowned as he was in the freedom it had promoted with regard to sex and drugs and art. But he had failed to identify the body which cast that shape. In doing so, he was astonished at how little interest he had taken before in the wonder of this world and what he had been thinking and how he was living, so much of which had been decided by these acts and these people.

The 1960s changed the world without doubt. The door to mainstream thinking was being kicked, if not down, then very much open. This was shown in the way that science, neoliberal capitalism and atheism were able to walk through this doorway to people's mass consciousness without the resistance they had previously faced.

In the rapid rise of previously marginalised or underground cultural movements and the increase in cross-cultural communications about beliefs and theologies, there was left in the wake of the idealism and violent confusion of the sixties a need for solidity and tangibility. The logic of scientific studies was often portrayed as the ultimate source of truth, emphasising data and evidence as the ground for our conclusions about life, rather than speculation or instinct. It was external, not internal, and at a time when people's internal worlds were confused, science had increased leverage as a solution to the problem of previously stable and isolated systems that now seemed to be disintegrating.

There has been no war, or any obvious key moment in the shift of mainstream attitudes away from patriarchal religion in the west, but instead there has been a silent but tangible creep of previously banned and 'immoral' activities being considered more and more acceptable. Sexuality, revealing outfits, swearing and violence are increasingly evident in the popular arena in music and art, for example, whilst money-laundering, drug use, and materialist ideology have become prominent in other areas of society. Rates of abortion and divorce have increased and children born to parents who are not married, for example, are no longer referred to as 'bastards', as they had been in previous generations.

Carrick was aware of all this. He had seen protests on the news and heard people speaking about the abandonment of religion every now and again, but nothing he had taken real notice of. Now, he saw he was a part of it, as it was a part of a wider picture too.

Alongside the increasing prevalence and acceptability of behaviours considered unacceptable by most major religions, church attendance in many countries has dropped. He read reports on surveys of contemporary religious beliefs to find out what was going on at the time and saw – to his complete lack of surprise – that the number of people following set religions of one kind or another had been decreasing. Meanwhile, the number of people who expressed belief in something but did not align themselves with any single religion was the largest growing sector of belief in the west.

Science is different to other belief systems' threat to established theologies. It is not simply another theory of the world. It is not simply another version of the same idea: it requires the shift of emphasis away from what simply makes sense to what could be proven. If science were to become the basis for our thinking, it would bring to an end the series of beliefs that have resulted from the assumption, made all those centuries ago, that there is something, somewhere else which created and has power over the world.

Carrick put down his books. He looked confusedly at them. Scattered across the floor, they seemed like an art work. He could see, and knew from his own life experience, that the world was moving to a more practical way of seeing things, and that there needed to be an end to all the bloodshed, the hatred, the justification for the abuse of independent thinkers, of ourselves and the minds of children, which had been permitted by beliefs about non-physical entities. They were incomprehensibly sad to him.

Yet he was still not happy – he knew science was not the answer, but another turning point in a maze of ways of being. He knew there was more to life than what he could see and touch with his body. He had seen and touched it with something other than hands and eyes, and felt its wonder inside him as he sat still, waiting for clarity once again.

In truth, Carrick resented scientific ways of thinking since his experience of dying. As he looked at his life, he saw that before his death he had used science in the same way as he claimed, with great disdain, religious people would use their beliefs, and that without realising it he had been just like them. He existed peacefully in the assumption that some scientists out there, somewhere, knew what they were doing, and used this idea to excuse him from ever looking at the world with his own eyes. This was just how religious believers looked to their vicars or rabbis to guide them, trusting that they knew the way and that they would never have to find their own path. It was an attitude of which scientific people spoke with a patronising sense of superiority. He also used scientific beliefs – or what he had been told they were – to make sense of his life and to help him cope with it when it was all too much. The thought that there was nothing more to his being than a single and arbitrary life had become like a sedative that eased him: it all meant nothing and is destined to end in emptiness so he did not need to worry. It was the concept of heaven in another language: he had been a religious person collapsing in the arms of a deity, except that it was a vacuum instead of a form.

In this way, science was not a new way of thinking about things at all; it was another religion to Carrick's mind now. It was hard, this existence called living, and we all had something which we used to get us through, and to deal with the emotions we find difficult to identify, let alone articulate or resolve – even scientists. Indeed, the laws of physics and biology and chemistry bore a passing resemblance to tenets of belief or commandments. Should a person experience an aspect of life which goes against these laws, such as the paranormal or spiritual, they are to feel guilt, repent and realign themselves with the way of thinking that is totally ordained by the mainstream, and apply themselves with greater diligence and vigour to the proper way of understanding life.

The use of the founding fathers of science, as with religion, to support what would clearly have been opposed by them is another point that upset Carrick. For example, he had seen that Jesus had spoken messages of love in the Holy Bible, but his name had been used to justify the Crusades and many other acts of violence. In the same way, he observed how Albert Einstein, who valued imagination over knowledge, became admired as one of the greats of scientific thinking, and how science valued knowledge over the imagination.

The scientifically purported idea that there is nothing more to life than what we can detect with our senses is currently fuelling fundamental changes in our ways of living. It has become used as a reference for capitalist, consumerist and self-destructively nihilistic behaviour. According to this way of thinking, what science shows is that we live and then die: nothing more. This results in the idea of a life without consequences, in which no one really matters. This philosophical outlook permits us to harm our ecosystem, not to mention each other and ourselves, through the unspoken assumption that no one will have to deal with the consequences of their own actions, and so it is not necessary to consider their impact. A lack of care is being shown toward the world as a result of such thinking.

Carrick's experience beyond had shown him very much the opposite: there really was life beyond death, and any idea that one can live without consequence, can destroy at will, and harm without repercussion is mistaken. The most surprising thing in all his looking was the sheer amount of logical, solid evidence Carrick found for his experiences in the afterlife, which were looked upon with doubt and almost hatred by nearly all parties of contemporary thought. Religions did not want to know about the evidence of life after death investigations because it seemed to suggest other structures to life than that which their particular set of beliefs propagated, such as their versions of Hell and Heaven. Science did not want to know about anything at all other than death.

At the heart of the argument was the idea which all experiences of the paranormal and non-physical point towards: the idea that we are eternal, energetic beings. Many professional psychiatrists, respected academics, and other such scientifically-minded people have worked in this field of research and spoken of the distinct and powerful possibility that such a supposedly left-field concept is a reality.

Carrick knew it was more than possible, and yet there was never a headline on a single newspaper which had read: 'Eternal Life Could Be Real' or even 'Top Scientists: Actually, Maybe Religious Believers Were Right, Maybe We Do Have Spirits.'

Subliminally, such ideas are rubbished in the mainstream, being as it is, obsessed with materialism and the body, trends and fads and the physical world. If this were all just a drop in a never-ending river of time and experience then these things would be ridiculous to think of – one's weight and taxes and car prices and so on – but expanding horizons to the point where time means nothing and problems are temporary ultimately leads to the idea, once pushed far enough, that nothing much really matters. This does not sell. It allows people to be freer and more peaceful, able to enjoy themselves in their never-ending, constantly evolving experience of who they are. People who now are said to have and to mean 'little' would one day be rulers. It would no longer be an overall system of good-bad, powerful-weak, talented-useless polarities created as a result of single-life mentalities.

Carrick saw that this was the next important domino to fall once we acknowledge the possibility of a spirit able to survive the body at death. Power, at the moment, is deemed a currency related to money and strength and fear, and usually masculinity. Were we to realise that we reincarnate and inevitably develop, we would have to re-assess our whole value system, and our current ideas, the outcomes of millennia of thinking about power in terms of the physical world, would instantly be made redundant. We would have to make a new version of the world and ourselves. Thus, some would feel that they had lost something, and had been mistaken for all of history, and this is not something we find easy to do. We would rather use every technique we have to continue living as we do, so we can think that it is all still working as it always has done. Also, those who aren't in any way suffering currently would not be challenged. It would take serious change to assimilate the ideas of recurring life into many belief systems, and the fear of legitimacy could lead to avoidance. If they could only see that it is not a failure to change, and that the evolution of the human species is at stake, Carrick thought, as he looked through the books which he used to despise so fervently, with surreal ecstasy.

The only ideas which spoke to Carrick were abstract beliefs concerning love and only love, and a unifying spirit of peace to life. This was very beautiful to him, yet such theories were so wishy-washy and infantile! They could not agree on a foundation amongst themselves, and many accounts left their speakers open to derision simply through their idealism and naivety. Yes, it was all very well, to speak of love and only love, but in a world full of war and suffering it simply antagonised a lot of people.

He concluded, after all his studying, that in the contemporary world there were three broad strands to human thinking: religious beliefs, scientific/atheistic beliefs, and the love-and-care-for-each-other humanist/uncertainty beliefs of not being sure anymore – Carrick knew where he stood. This third group could perhaps be considered as the people lost somewhere in-between science and spirituality. As these two huge, mass plates of theological ground split apart, it appeared that many people were falling in the gap opening up between them, not believing in nothing at all, but not sure about any particular set of beliefs.

At this point in his journey of discovering his own true biography through reading that of the world, Carrick found another of his questions answered. He finally understood why he had thought as he had, why he had avoided all beliefs, and he forgave himself for not wanting to find out more. After all, there was a lot of threat involved; people made him feel as if should he look at the issue and establish a point of view, one that was liable to upset people no matter what it was. If he were an atheist, he was going to hell, if he were a member of a certain religion, he was either deluded or had picked the wrong one, and if he believed there was something but was unsure what, he was a flower-power dreamer who should stay away from the hallucinogens. Everyone was upset about something; no one could be who they are and be loved by everyone for it, no matter what they thought life was. It was very clear to him that it was a very confusing time to be alive – or, to put it more specifically, to consider what it is to be alive.

After his moment of comprehension, and the culmination of intensely looking at himself and this world, Carrick took a short break. He went out and socialised. And though he now was different in his own skin and the way he was around people, he found that he very much enjoyed himself. Deep down though, after a while, Carrick's sense of triumph faded. He tried not to feel this, to maintain the contentment of the understanding and compassion he had found for who he is and was and will be. But after a while he could not stop his transformation into an altogether less comfortable sort of emotional state. He was, yes, he was angry.

He began to see the dissolution of religion and scientific ways of thinking about life as resembling a giant, long-running, messy divorce, in which the lone child, neglected and used according to the parents' desire to harm one another, was truth itself. He saw that the outcome was that for children being born now, not to mention for the last several millennia, there simply was not a framework by which all could live happily. He saw that people are all being misled – from atheists to fundamentalists, and will be until someone comes up with an ideology in which there is no need for leaders and so people will be able to lead themselves. As long as people are told they need the world to be translated for them, they will always be abused and misled; and there is always a queue for such a position.

The people in control had been interested in power and not truth for too long, and he, along with presumably everyone else, was suffering in the to-ing and fro-ing of intolerant, stubborn, and aggressive ways of thinking. It became increasingly agonizing even to think about thinking, and the price of intellectual calm was ignorance.

It was clear to Carrick that the world needed a new way of seeing things, one that welcomed all knowledge, was broader, more encompassing, more concerned with truth than anything else. He then did something his former self would have baulked at: he decided that it would have to be he who made this new vision of the world.

As a logical, rational, and infuriated cohabitant on this planet, the opportunity was his. With all the information available, with the lack of fear of death that he had, with an insatiable desire to propel the truth forward amidst the agendas of people who were not interested in anyone but themselves, at a moment in time when religion and science and every way of thinking swayed on the spot, confused by what it was all figuring out, Carrick decided to put all these pieces of life's puzzle together and make the picture at last, reveal the image which currently lay fragmented in his lap. His motivation was simple: to make sure no one in the future could be blindfolded, spun around, and un-blindfolded as he had been.

ELEVEN

The Cockroaches or The Future (To Come to Light is to Flame Another and Another)

Angels and dreams and all unseen things
    Finding their ways past my boundaries and under my horizons
    Yet never brought before my eyes,
    Which keep blinding themselves with the understanding
    That they had never seen anything at all

What can I make of a world so changed?
    If change is all there is
    And all will ever be in a whirl of disassociation anyway

It's never alone to be
    But to be is a lonely thing
    Why is this, if we are all the same and think the same
    Or are told we should be doing so

We have long belonged to a past
    Which betrays who we are so greatly
    It is close, but should not overcome the inside
    For that should be kept open
    To whatever wants to fill you

In the moment you stand inside and fill also
So let yourself be filled,
And do not think, 'Oh but I will lose all that I have'
Because nothing is worth anything
Except that you were there and could feel what it was
To have happened as it had

Dragons and serpentines and cockroaches, too
These are beasts which prey upon the souls of young men and women
And never let go until they have made you like them too;
Ugly and diseased and intent upon hurting one another

It is all the same to be the same
In a place where people desire never to be themselves
They are never allowed what they will never be able to rid themselves of,
And live in torture because of this

It cannot happen
It cannot be allowed to happen
That we will eventually end by destroying the human race
When the world is so full of love and light and all we must do
Is take the blindfold off and forget the past

It was in frustration that he had begun to write the words he could not speak. His words sometimes barely made sense, looked out of place in the external world, and besides these sound reasons to object to his sharing them, he had been dishonest with the doctor from the word go. Therefore, he did not feel he had betrayed any trust or bond in writing these things, and continued to do so.

Each time we love
  We give ourselves a gift of epic proportions
  For each time we love
  We give to ourselves a love in return
  This takes time to understand
  But in the end
  The only person to love is ourselves
  And each other is just a by-product of this

He began writing in earnest, and soon became less inhibited by the need to give his words a structure, and out from deep within him came thought after thought to fill his pages: snatches, phrases, glimpses.

The opposite of vampires are those who live in life's shadows: the vampires are easily seen

The crux of normalcy is dishonesty

Reality is neither what it seems
Nor what it seems not

Heroes are for people who need them

Trying to find your centre is like trying to find the centre of the universe.

In the beginning of his relationship with the doctor, there had been a problem: Carrick no longer approved of being told how to live in any way. He did not believe anything anyone had ever told him or would tell him anymore, and so refused to engage at all with the idea of being healed with the help of another.

Whenever a day came when he decided to speak to the doctor, to try to be close to him, he bounded into the meeting room and found that the couch seemed decidedly harder than it had done previously. The coffee seemed weak and without flavour, the air stuffy and sickly scented. He perched uncomfortably on his chair with a disdainful look on his face, and when the Doctor asked him a question, Carrick would mumble the same awkward answers that he always provided in response – something about being 'okay'. He did not like the reason why he was there, or how he had come to be in this situation. Even if it had been a much more peaceable affair between the two of them, Carrick still would have found it difficult to express the reality of the sensations he had felt at death's touch. His experience had been richer than he could ever convey, so he did not want even to try.

Deep down, Carrick felt that a therapist was not the right kind of person with whom to speak about these things, such real and heartfelt things that require risk and bravery and the receiving of empathy in order for the tear of exposure not to scar. He had misled the doctor with a story about a near-death experience that he had read in some books.

Carrick thought this was acceptable. The reason for this was that there was a cause and an effect he approved of. He hated driving home now, hated people trying to overtake him on the inside, and the cause was his accident, it having involved such dramatic collisions between not only his physical being and the outside world, but also his inner self and a whole other place altogether. The effect of manipulating the doctor was that it stopped any more collisions, this time between his inside world and the outside. It was too much for him, and sometimes he would say, 'No more, please, no more', as if to the air in an abstract expression of despair. He repeated phrases or pleas in a trance until he felt that somehow they had been received by the elements which governed him.

The way in which even this fabricated version of events for the Doctor had incurred such concern left him wondering just how bland one had to make one's life before it was not disturbing to anyone anymore. It was a quite impossible task proving yourself sane, and so in silent rooms, judged by no one, he would sit inside a ring of fire and truth so that he may feel that which he had really experienced: he could not express that in words, he simply felt it.

Sometimes, however, he felt that he could try at least to verbalize it.

TWELVE

"Doctor Turnstone."

"Yes?"

"What would you say if I told you I have lied to you?"

There was a disconcerted pause.

"What have you lied to me about, Carrick?" the Doctor asked, more in curiosity than in concern, for he knew that whenever people have to converse with professionals about their emotions or mind, lying can often feel a sensible option.

"Well, the truth of my experience of nearly dying."

"It was all made up?"

The Doctor was shocked.

"No, it was the truth, but just the truth of other people, and possibly some other things as well". He looked embarrassed. "I haven't told you anything about my truth at all because I was scared to say it. I had no idea who you were. And I was trying to recover from my family having found me strange in what I told them, which wasn't very much…" He trailed off. "But I am growing to believe that each time a person gives, they give to themselves really, and so I think I should tell you what really happened. I feel that I have betrayed myself in betraying you."

"Well, I don't think it is quite that bad, but it would be good to learn what has happened," he said. "I want to help you, Carrick."

"I know," Carrick acknowledged. "I'll tell you then, if you'd like?"

"Yes. Very much."

"Well," he took a deep, long, breath. "I did die," Carrick stated in a manner that was not at all dramatic, "but I didn't feel the way I said about dying. It wasn't heaven. It was not hell but it was not heaven. I wish it had been and I could say that it was all true..."

He looked sad.

"But it was unlike anything you have ever dreamt of. I could not have imagined that place until I actually experienced it. When I died, I saw that each part of life was important. Each person, word and choice had a consequence and changed the future of others. Yet it was also less real than when I had been alive – this chair, this table, this lamp, these people," he flicked a hand towards a window, "they are not really here as such."

"How can that be?"

"Just in the same way that I am not really me – I am many things: I am the night, the day, the sun, the rain. Nothing is really as it seems. It is all an experience I am choosing to have, simply because I can; because it is a good thing to have, a real gift."

The words were a gift to the doctor, as well. He was interested in learning all he could of this place.

"So you are dead. Explain to me how you have come to reach this conclusion, what it is like? How have you come to see the life you have as unreal?"

"In life, we are limited by things like time and space. But in death it is different. There are physical aspects but it is not the same as in this life..."

"But there was something?"

"Yes, of course there was something. It could never end this thing called existence. Everything was so clear. The first thing that happened was that the world as I had known it faded. I felt surrounded by love and was filled with peace."

"Was anyone there?"

"No..."

"So what happened then – anything at all?"

"Oh yes – lots of things! It's so hard to explain. I stayed until I felt a part of that realm, and was at peace with myself. Then it started to change. The only way to articulate it is that forms started to shape themselves. This mass of light became scenes, with laughter and crying, all different, but I recognised what they had been: they were the scenes of my life. They surrounded me like a wall of sound and vision, and I tried to control them and make them stop but I had no power to do so. Their purpose was to make me understand what I had done, the consequences of every part of what I had chosen to do to people and to life."

"And how was it for you, that realisation in total fullness if you don't mind me asking?"

"It was absolutely unendurable."

"WHY?"

"Because always there was so much friction between what I could be and what I was. The choices I made were so unspeakably awful, and all I could have been was just beside me. I was never completely realised, though. And then I became terrified..."

"In what sense?" the doctor asked, although his honest response would have been empathy.

"I just was… horrible."

There stood a sheet of time which they both had to walk across before they could start speaking again. Carrick continued, shivering a little from the stress of recalling it all.

"I had no idea who that person was. I was vile. But the beauty – or the potential for beauty – always remained in every moment, and in realizing that only once I had left it, I became tortured by having not chosen to seize it, to make the most of it. It was clear what I had not done: to have loved others as I could, as I would have liked them to have loved me. I had no idea how to treat people, what to do, how to live. I had no aim in life except to follow others. I was suffocated by the awareness that I had not really known anything about myself. Then something else, something extraordinary, began happening..."

He stopped himself, unable to convey that event in language. He continued knowing that he had spoken only half-truths and had so far belied himself and his story. He would not do so again, he could not keep making this mistake. He was going to say it, however it was received; it was never up to him anyway.

"...two questions were addressed to me, and they came from the same essence or element which had filled me and that now surrounded me. Just as the shapes and sensations had arisen previously, these questions just filled me. It was something more essential than breath, from what would have been lungs: it was as if all that is and has ever been was being shown to me. It was able to speak to me. It said that it held the two questions of life and that I had to answer truthfully.

"The two questions of life," Doctor Turnstone heard himself reiterate. "The first question was: 'Have you learned yet?' and I replied, 'learned what? LEARNED WHAT?' And it said; 'To love.' And inside I felt myself answer, it just echoed, 'No.' I could not answer any other way. I became sadder than I had ever been in life, and then it continued with another question: 'In your life, how have you made the world a better place?'

"It was as if all I was ached for mercy. I just knew... I just knew... I could see... that I had done virtually nothing, absolutely nothing, to help make the world a better place. I had just absorbed the world's messages and even though I had seen suffering, I had never stood up to say how I believed the world should be – more loving, more open, more truthful..."

The psychiatrist was being held in the arms of these words, but Carrick had returned to that state and felt that same lonely ache, and continued no more. He began to cry. There was no effort from either of them to hurry the emotion, and Carrick lay his head gently back in his chair and let his tears fall down, at last letting another see them.

THIRTEEN

The act of watching his patient's tears fall, without trying to stop them or explain them away, changed the nature of the doctor's relationship to Carrick. It became more than simply a professional interaction. They were drawn closer, they were entwined as human beings, and a love between the two of them began to grow.

Carrick continued as best he could.

"...and then suddenly I was back, and all I wanted was to understand how this could have happened – how we could have let ourselves do this, how we could have let people think any other way? I had destroyed the innocence I was born with, something precious beyond measure. All I had ever done was try to get things that I could not take with me when I died, and try to please people who could not go with me. They never cared what I carried inside because of them. Just as when I felt and saw and touched where we go, I can still see that everywhere there is only unconsciousness, unconsciousness, unconsciousness, and I want to bring it all to an end."

There was a feeling of anger in the room which was palpable to the professional doctor.

"End?" the doctor thought to himself, who was unwilling or unable to bring to an end Carrick's denial of this world. Yet there was something about this tale which was puzzling him: the way in which his patient had spoken of the afterlife before had seemed stale to him, but when Carrick had really opened up, the doctor almost felt he had experienced something phenomenal himself. It was as if it were in the room with them, and that the light, or the darkness, he had seen was somehow carried inside him. On such occasions the Doctor was not sure if it could all be simply in the mind, as he felt it reaching out towards him.

The clinician's natural reaction was to doubt, and he came up with ten arguments to disallow the possibility that this quality Carrick manifested could be real. First, he considered what the options were for a scientific explanation: drug hallucinations, brain haemorrhages, religious fantasies too realistic for the logical mind to interpret sensibly.

Carrick's case was interesting, however. He was not a drug taker, and the way in which he had died worked against the plausibility of some alternative theories: in medical terms, he had died almost instantly on the motorway, and had been resuscitated in the ambulance. That was already something extraordinary. The notes made at the time by the paramedics recorded him claiming to have been spoken to by what he called 'love'.

And the doctor found more fascinating information in those medical notes. Carrick had spoken intensely about the experience to a nurse called Henry. She noted him claiming that he had only come to life in the last few hours, and that before he had been dead inside: "Full of fear and anticipation of things which would never have arrived anyway!"

This echoed what Carrick had told him, that he felt he had somehow 'called the experience towards himself', because he had not known what he was doing, and had wanted to make himself see. But the doctor was still unsure as to what was true and what was false, because once a person has been shown to have lied it places a considerable question mark over their further utterances.

It was starting to make more sense to the doctor, however, as to how his patient could have been so disturbed by what had happened. Before that, there had been only the physical side effect of having been unable to sleep since the accident, which suggested that there had been some severe feeling of distress provoked by the experience. This sleep-deprivation had been dismissed by Carrick – he had been kept awake by the need to understand the experience. As an explanation, this seemed sufficient to him.

In terms of the external evidence for this kind of experience, then, it was difficult to disprove Carrick. The ambulance crew reported that he had displayed no brain activity on their arrival, and so any theory that his synapses were firing randomly could be ruled out. He was not a religious man, and did not have any prior inclination toward spirituality, as evidenced by his own account of himself and those of his close friends and family.

In short, there was no physical explanation, and no emotional reason for why Carrick would have wanted to have such an experience. There was no reward for him in the kind of behaviour and words it had elicited and it could only be assumed therefore that he believed in them, that he had been genuinely afraid to speak the entirety of his experience before a relationship basis had been formed. This would make sense to the doctor, and only further encouraged the idea that Carrick really had had an experience along the lines of what he was claiming.

What people believe has happened to them and what actually happened can be different, though, and the doctor continued to probe for alternative explanations rather than to address it as a reality.

Carrick, however, had a burning fire of passion in him these days, and would not be contained within the explanations the doctor offered him: it had been a real experience of a real place. After a while, however, problems became apparent. What the doctor hadn't foreseen was just how many of life's obstacles Carrick would attempt to navigate; the number of diverging paths he would walk down and turn back from, only to start all over again from the same spot of admitting that he did not know what life was about. It was only a small amount of time before cracks began to emerge in Carrick's portrayal of himself as a questing, diplomatic assessor of The Truth. A façade which gleamed on the outside was inevitably painful and ugly on the inside.

The doctor was reminded of times in his life when he had tried to do the same, but had run away from what he was uncovering. It truly scared him to see how little people know of life, and it was a realisation he shied away from. But he could never find a way to see things differently.

His appointments with Carrick were a challenge; no one else came to his office with such thoughts or questions. Most people were too exhausted from trying to help themselves – too dragged down by their own burdens, too scarred by their own particular set of wounds – to consider helping other people. Maybe Carrick was like this too, but just could not see it.

Eventually, the need to get to his own truths and those of humanity became Carrick's only concern, he sat in the night watching balls of gas burn in a dark sky, destroying themselves to be noticed. 'Suns cannot see that among which they shine', he thought, how 'worthy' or capable it is of receiving gifts of light, and what such gifts will do to those who feel its force. Planets are held in awe of suns' powers, but what holds the suns in their places? He empathised with their desires, unconscious and natural, and also wanted to shine. All his past life was fuel with which he was going to ignite just like them, be immovable as they were with all revolving around them.

He was also going mad inside his walls of skin and hair and teeth and muscles, because this is what happens when a person has a lifetime of emotional hatred, violence and mixed messages heaped upon his or her emotional self, it leaves you as a corpse in a lavish burial vault. Carrick sensed that if he could only climb out of this hole and bring these treasures up to life's surface he would be a rich and free man indeed. For he knew that there is nothing a person in pain cannot do if she or he might only unwrap such gifts.

But he began to struggle at what was just too much for him. He had no alternative but to keep trying to get to a finishing point which did not exist, as someone training for a marathon knows the circle he is running upon will never end. The doctor always kept an eye out for such problems, of course. Alert and aware, and reading between the lines of Carrick's script on each visit, even within his most profound insights and probing, the doctor was conscious of watching someone thrashing away far from shore in a deep sea. It was an image which regularly came to him when he thought of his patient – to die and come back must be an overwhelming experience, and the way Carrick had not initially accepted it as such had worried him. To acknowledge you are in difficulty is the only way anyone can heal after such events, and too often Carrick had seemed someone trying to take a traumatic experience in his stride. The doctor knew the house of cards that was denial and delusion in the human mind. So he found it interesting to see Carrick swipe his hand against collective structures, whilst seemingly unaware he stood at the apex of his own.

This was not uncommon with those who accepted what they heard without questioning, and Carrick, in spite of a growing scepticism which the doctor had attempted to instil in him, was always ingesting so much more than he could possibly handle emotionally. He had no respect for himself or his own problems.

Such was the second point of concern for the doctor.

Initial denial of the severity of his experiences, followed by intellectual over-reaching: with shaky foundations and over-ambitious plans for the building, the house of Carrick's mind threatened to collapse.

FOURTEEN

'No one cares. How can I live in a world like this?' Carrick often asked himself this kind of question on this kind of day. He began to visit religious centres which just sent him spinning out in cartwheels of inner rage. But nevertheless they comforted him in ways he could not remember being able to accept in his old self. It was just a feeling of something more than him: that was enough for Carrick.

That was all he wanted.

Time passed.

The Doctor said, "I hear you're going to Church these days."

"Yes."

"Does it help you?"

"I'm not really sure…"

"Good. How are you feeling in general at the moment?"

"Bad."

"Why?"

"I'm lonely."

"But I'm here, Carrick! You can talk to me."

But Carrick did not want to talk anymore. All aspirations for progress in his life had now left him, just as he had desired. Everything was just making him sadder and lonelier and more isolated from everyone else.

One week he simply did not want to talk anymore at all. He turned up to an appointment with the doctor, sat down with the familiar faraway look in his eyes, but this time, unusually, he had no explanation for why it was there. He just sat quietly, making only polite gesticulations or, if forced to talk, he would reply monosyllabically. But he was really not himself: he knew not what to say.

Before the next session, Carrick called to say that he didn't feel he could make it in. His soft voice was distant, and then... nothing. The doctor contacted Carrick's father when he also failed to show up at the next session. He feared something terrible. His father broke the news that Carrick, the doctor's friend and patient, had been taken to a local psychiatric hospital that morning.

When he went to visit Carrick, Paul felt a lump in his throat. He was crying in the car on the way there: he had failed in what he had been trying to do with Carrick, for he had been trying to make him well. He reproached himself bitterly and wept the blood of the self-slain.

As he approached the gateway, there was an ominous cloud-line overhead, ceasing as the grounds of the hospital did at the far away end, and the intense nausea he felt within him was his only clear focus. He aggressively rebalanced himself, stepped inside the glass door and went up the marble stairs.

The staff there knew him well. He had never taken personally the number of his patients who had been admitted there, but it was still a heart-breaking experience each and every time. Carrick looked very much as the others had: changed, drawn, withdrawn – a hollow vision of his former self.

"Hello, Carrick," the doctor greeted him, with a smile of sincerity and well-wishing.

Carrick did not respond.

"How are you?"

A look from beyond was in Carrick's eyes, and no words could call it back. Seeing that inner turmoil, the doctor began to engage with him in a one-way, condoning manner. He tried not to be patronising and stayed for longer than was necessary to make sure his care was in evidence to Carrick. It was normal for someone to be this way: in losing their sanity there was often a raw, bleeding wound of shame and confusion which left many people unable to comprehend the change in their life – and silence eased this. Sometimes, patients could be responsive, but the combination of a very sensitive mind and a shaken inner structure meant that the doctor's anticipation had been mute. He had assessed in advance the way Carrick would be, that this would happen.

His patient had once explained to the doctor in happier times that he believed a person's spirit can be more or less present according to what they are thinking. If a person thinks of yesterday, for example, a part of themselves will detach itself from where they are in the present. He believed that if you have a very active mind, as his had become, highly energized and dancing to mad rhythms, you can go all over the place without something to hold you down.

With no one besides the doctor able to help him in these visits to far-away places, Carrick had drifted deep into the outer reaches of his mind. He was soon no longer present in the here and now.

Carrick's belief in souls and their whereabouts were not shared by the doctor, but the latter very much knew about the mind and how to identify its clarity and focus. He could tell from Carrick's state that, soul or no soul, his mind was in so many different places it was not able to be with him in those moments. He did not know where it was in terms of synapses or memory cells – or in the ether and time-fields that Carrick envisaged - but he wished it a speedy, safe return home all the same.

FIFTEEN

Unlike the doctor, Carrick had not seen this coming. In his return to life he had been reluctant, yet he had never foreseen the split in perception that would come: between here and elsewhere. He knew how precious it was to be here as well as elsewhere, and in his thinking he was trying to do something quite specific: he was trying to find a way to resolve his suffering and confusion.

And then he was here, pacing, scratching, cold, strange. But it was not him that was the problem! Everyone else – they were the problem! They wouldn't come with him! They wouldn't believe! They did not want to know what he had to know: why we're here!

It was the physical side of him that first suffered and, though he tried not to, he began to just sit around and neglect his family and friends. He did nothing but think about everything.

How was he to know that the inside and outside world were becoming separate once more, just as they had all those years ago? How was he to know that when he watched the ceiling peel away from him that this was not what was meant to happen when one is truly realised and released from life's cages? All he felt was splatters from the cosmos that sprayed across his mind. People came and offered him drinks but he spat out the offers and continued apace. Where he was going with this behaviour no one knew, least of all Carrick.

He refused to work yet found it embarrassing not to be a part of what most people are. He could see then that he had always been strange, that everyone else was too but to more or less degrees, and how he had previously been of the 'less' variety but circumstances had changed this to the 'more'. Sometimes he could be cruel and lack understanding. He would say to himself that he had given himself away for the price of others' acceptance, and hated what was left of him now. But then he would realise he was only human, and that the place where he had been was only a temporary home; he belonged here.

All those people who knew him never really liked him anyway, he could tell that even back then. There is something so visual and stark about fakery, which is why looking around in a crowded scene is so depressing. We *are all* giving ourselves over to this thing, he thought, this desire for acceptance, and as he contemplated this in despair, he was more and more determined not to 'be like them' again. Inevitably it detached him.

There was excitement in his liberation, however, and he grew strong in declaring his own weakness, or so he thought. Yet when he wasn't discovering new ideas or putting pieces together with the rate of success and clarity he felt was required, it was all he could do just to sit disturbed by his own emotional reflection, with which the mirror of time constantly seduced him. In such states he would conclude that after all this struggle he was only a sad, insecure mental case who had never had a clue how to live his life and probably never would have. Maybe what he wanted to say was that this was alright. If he could say one thing to the people of this world, to the entire whole world, to the hordes that had criticised and ridiculed him from his very first cry out of the womb, he would say this:

'You don't know either, and you never will. And that's okay, and if we admit that that's what's going on, and that that's alright, maybe we can be happier before we die, and see how no one ever knew and how we were always okay anyway. There's nothing to learn or to be, except to learn to be content in never being able to learn or be what we are not. The important thing is to learn to love ourselves, and to make ourselves happy, and therefore all we have to know is ourselves.'

Most religions and movements say that their way is the only way to be and that all others are wrong. But how can they be right, he realised, when no religion or idea of life had ever spoken to him as clearly as his own confusion? They never mention human error in religions, or the changing of minds, or the growing that comes from such things. They would never permit the release of every single person's own unique ways of doing things. And such things, it became shiningly clear and stark to Carrick, were truth.

Obviously, he did not see how his focus was shifting itself away from everyone else's idea of reality. It does not work like that in the mind – everyone thinks they are sane and normal, it all makes sense to us or we wouldn't do what we do. In the hospital, Carrick took time to reflect on the past year. His accident had been both his blessing and his curse. He was now relaxed and did not fear death or pain or anything else. Yet what he found out was just how fearful people are, and that without this fear, he now had little in common with any of them. Too often, they were working because they feared losing their house, they systematically made friends in fear of isolation, they calculated their style of dress to impress others, rather than to express who they were. It had been truly disturbing to look at his own life and see the same things in himself, but to carry on like that was not an option anymore.

Thus, he found himself sitting here, on a psychiatric hospital corridor, still trying to figure out a way he could save the world without destroying himself in the process. Maybe he had failed, and it was too late – this was one intellectual cloud which crept over his mental horizon too closely, raining its contents down upon his heart when it was too full to hold in anymore. 'Maybe I'll be resigned to this forever, never knowing anyone again, or even wanting to.' He consciously bled, he was torn open, and he had to catch the blood, and quickly.

But his head was not working overtime for nothing, and he began to write down what he was thinking. Working through and then reassessing as he went along, everything was checked and re-checked, debated and re-formulated. He could see which pieces fitted where, and the previously unworkable puzzle was raised from the mess in his lap. It began to form itself so wholly in front of Carrick's eyes that it took him aback. Working on it in the recreation room which others seldom visited, he amassed a great stack of papers, madly scribbled upon, and eventually asked the nurses if he could use the office computer to type it up.

Miracles have impeccable timing, and having observed his dedication, and being convinced of its worth to him, the nurses made an exception to every pretentious rule the hospital strove to uphold, and moved an old computer out into the room he worked in. It was the best gift Carrick could remember receiving, and two months before his six month sentence of incarceration was up, he had actually finished a manuscript. Changed again, he felt worn out, beaten, his hair scraggly and wild, with a beard he had trouble keeping in control. His flesh had melted, but physical appearances were again a misrepresentation of what lay within. And he felt the contentment of the fulfilled was glowing within him as he put the finished copy on his bedside table. The top sheet was blank, but for the title.

The Religion of Self-Enlightenment

Carrick Ares

A Conversation about Belief

If you put two people from alternate regions of the world in a room together and tell them they may speak, but only of the weather, they may find that one of them likes the sun better, while the other prefers snow. They may even find the differences between their views interesting. They would probably not fight over their differing opinions. Yet if you asked them to discuss their beliefs about life, there is a much higher chance that they would find something to argue about. One of them might even try to physically harm the other to prove something about the sun or snow.

This is a metaphor for the danger of human beliefs and it is not acceptable to continue like this. It is known that each person has a unique combination of ideas and beliefs which have been mixed together through their experience of life. If someone has been brought up in nature by parents who shielded them from civilization, for example, it is unlikely that they will become Muslim. There is a crucial link between the many belief systems which dominate the world, and that is their intolerance. They cannot accept that people might have their own ideas, and argue constantly about that which binds them all – what it is to be alive, and what happens afterward. And there are many sub-divisions of such beliefs, many sticking points to provoke hatred and intolerance, with each reducing the possibility of peace for the world.

There are several things which cause this ideological aggression, which must be discussed and brought to an end if the human race wishes for such ways of thinking no longer to plague it. The first of these points of discussion is the most obvious: the specific words and terminology that religious belief employs.

The Language of Belief

There is something about the language of belief which reduces experience to broad concepts split into polar terms, alongside a manipulation of indefinable words. People use words to understand their world. Spoken and written communication, however, can be more problematic than silence in some ways: a person can talk of physical things and be roughly comprehended by another, but only roughly. Should two people witness the same robbery, as police reports show, they will recount two versions of the same event. Things get even more problematic when people try to discuss beliefs. The main reason for the difficulty is the use of inner concepts of life and abstract terms: truth, goodness, love, evil, sin, holiness, spirit and more. Words such as these are the very lexicon of belief. The definitions of them affect global culture. However, these terms have no set definitions, and they are all paired with insulting opposites with no middle ground.

People have invented such concepts and words. This means that they can never be defined in purely concrete or fixed terms. However, when speaking of them people make no mention of their individual ability to define them; everyone speaks of 'goodness' and 'sin' and all the other terms as if they have found the absolute definitions, but the very status of the words as abstract nouns or adjectives means that they can have no such categorical interpretation.

The potential for harm here is seen, to give one example, in the way in which many destructive activities such as war are redefined through linguistic terminologies so they appear at least to have a claim to be 'good'. It is the broadness of such key words that makes this possible. This aspect of human language, with regard to belief, is constantly abused by people with a vested interest in keeping public opinion on their side, or in getting a large number of people to do as they suggest.

There are many kinds of truth, all wrapped up in a single word. The first and most basic definition of truth is that which agrees with fact. For example, if a person is shown a blue pencil, and when asked what it is, says it is a blue pencil, this would be true. A second meaning of the word 'truth' is to do with people's internal beliefs, however, which cannot be seen or verified as easily. If a devout Christian were asked if Jesus Christ is the Son of God, they would say that this is 'true'. If an atheist were asked if there was no God, they would say that this was 'true', there is no God. This is belief not fact. There are therefore two key aspects to truth: that which is external and factual, and that which is internal and belief.

This sheds light on the central problem: that human beings have to use identical terms when speaking of external and internal truth, knowing full well that they are different things. This is what leaves people so prone to arguing. Anyone who describes a 'blue pencil' as a 'rhinoceros' and claims this to be true has made a mistake because there are objective references for set terms like these. Beliefs, however, have no such objective terms, so if beliefs clash there is no objective framework to hold up against them. Arguments can then only be resolved by means other than logic.

This yoking of beliefs and fact within the one term, 'truth', has been disastrous for humanity. For one example, it was once 'true' that the world was flat, and not round. This was not 'true' in the sense of fact, but because it was believed to be fact at the time, it was considered to be 'true'.

Such broad usage means that the term 'truth' can be associated with very strange ideas, smuggled in under the guise of accuracy, honesty, adherence to general opinion and so forth. Once things that are actually belief are held to be fact, they are considered inarguable. They are protected by being included in the same linguistic category as that which is totally inarguable.

Many worthwhile ideas which do not align with a particular theory held to be 'truth' are immediately summarily dismissed. This highlights the second characteristic of these abstract, yet central and vital terms, which is that they are poled with negative opposites in a black or white manner, and with an absence of descriptive terms for the grey in between.

If something is not 'good', it must be therefore 'bad'. It cannot be 'not good' and still not be 'bad'; the only word we have for this is the colloquial idea of it being 'okay' – which is only a dismissal of the matter at hand. This too, then, leads to aggression, for if someone says Islam is 'okay' or tolerable it will offend a Muslim. When something has been classified as 'right', 'true' or 'good' by a culture, then everything that opposes it is at risk of being labelled 'wrong', 'false' or 'bad', even though it might be completely true.

The definition of words is secretly the most fought-over of all issues. After something has been determined to be truth by whatever means – violence, persuasion or simply an idea's originality – it is then that logic comes into play. After the initial building blocks of truth have been laid in place, therefore, people use formulae or syllogisms to elaborate deductions from them. They say:

I know this is so and this is so, therefore this is or is not so.

Aside from violence and brutality, there is also then a logical structure to help people decide on their truths, the A+B=C approach to defining our ideas. For example:

This colour is the colour blue + I see a car that is that colour = that car is blue.

If this person were to say that the car was red, he would then be lying, because he understands the criteria, and it can only be a blue car as a result of them. Yet this logic can become more complex:

I was born in Hungary and have lived here all my life + the natives of this land are called Hungarians = I am Hungarian

If this person claimed to be Russian, however, it is not absolutely certain they are not telling the truth as well – perhaps their family was from Russia and they consider this their true place of origin, or they have changed nationality. This means that how they describe themselves is to some extent at their own discretion, and is also dependent on the attitudes of those listening, who may question this 'truth' if presented as different to their own ideas on nationhood and race and so on.

Given that the initial inputs for beliefs are often decided by force and not by intellectual worth, there is very little chance that we are getting this right with things people cannot touch or feel or physically prove.

The system of working through truth and beliefs is no longer working and so it is being abandoned, allowing things which do not make sense to exist simply because people believe they could do. For example, many years ago if a person used given A's and B's to discern C's it may have been feasible that:

We are unable to know what happens outside of our tribe or village + people are born and die = perhaps people come from other places and go to these places after they die.

This was a logical assumption, and may feasibly have been true in a factual sense. Having formulated a 'C' then, they may try and establish where this place is and what it looks like, every single region in the world having a different theory about this realm.

For example:

There is a place people come from and go to + we have brown skin and look a certain way = this place is the home of the creators of humanity who are similar to us yet are even more amazing.

This would have made sense. But there are problems with the formula now because the results of this process, the 'C's which have been produced and expanded upon considerably by now, have been declared 'absolute truth' and not 'our idea of truth at the moment'. They become entwined with actual fact in a linguistic sludge, and therefore, as time has gone on, these C's have been challenged, but will not be changed easily.

Some, therefore, have come up with the following formula (which is very popular after centuries of battling to decide the C of all C's, or the God of all Gods):

Many people believe in different deities + they then harm one another in their deities' names = belief in deities is harmful, thus they should all be abandoned.

Once again, this 'C' then becomes a truth and is intermingled with 'facts' to become an 'A' or a 'B' of subsequent formulas, resulting in yet more 'C's'.

God does not exist + there is evidence of life after death = the evidence of life after death is wrong.

This, once more, is a result of input claimed to be more than that: ideas declared facts and not beliefs.

If ten oranges are laid out and one is picked out as being very 'good', the others are not thrown away. But if ten ideas about life are laid out and one is said to be the 'truth', the others become 'lies' immediately, even if they are almost identical in shape and form. The person picking out that belief may want to say, 'All of them are true and interesting and relevant, but I feel this to be the most true from the way I see things'. In the language of belief, there are no words for such opinions.

The only solution is to reconfigure the idea of what words mean and how people should try to use them: more carefully, more clearly, and with less polarity. In the same way that words are at the root of many actions, it is 'truth' that is the one word at the centre of all of this. Every term regarding good and bad, right and wrong, and so forth, must spring from some notion of 'truth', and it is obvious that there is a link between the abstract nature of theological terminology and its claim to truth. That which is deemed 'true' has a concrete element because of its association with material facts, and this is the only aspect to any belief which is physical and has a claim to solidity. This is the seed from which beliefs tend to grow.

Primarily, then, there must be a separation of internal facts from external facts. Rather than deeming those who disagree with one's ideas of truth to be 'liars', which incites passionate reactions, it might be better simply to insert the word 'personal' before any idea of truth.

There is thereby no need for contrasting views to become, merely by conflict with one person's interpretation of truth, 'lies' or 'wrong' - they are simply another truth as defined by another person. Two people can have different personal truths and no one has the right to call another person's version of the truth 'lies'.

Alongside the distinction between fact and personal truth, there is another prominent distinction: between personal truth and absolute truth. Here too, the mixture of beliefs and fact, and the vagueness of the word 'truth', means that people speak of their personal truth as if it were eternal truth; objective, all-knowing, inarguable. This is because no distinction is made between 'personal truth' and 'absolute truth'.

There is a relationship between the two but they are clearly not the same thing. An image can be made to clarify the differences: there are infinite roads of personal truth, all leading to absolute truth.

Such a way of thinking of the relationship between personal and absolute truth, after separating them out, instantly removes the conflict between the terms. People are all on their individual roads, and so why fight to decide the path to take?

Shifting an internally created idea back to an inner source is the only reasonable solution. Every external fact that has ever been posited must have once been an internal fact. For example, Sir Isaac Newton became aware of gravity when he watched an apple fall to the ground from a tree and propelled the concept from his inner world to explain this having happened. Truth comes from within in its purest sense.

There are external facts of many kinds, however. Everyone is looking to provide them, from religious institutions to governments to schools to neighbours. They all want people to build their pathways with the paving stones they have given them. This is because in accepting another's fact as building material, people are purchasing it with what that which many people value in the external world: power. This is the currency of the exchange of facts.

Some people have good intentions, however. When a mother teaches her child not to run in the road she is not looking to harvest that child's power, but to plant a seed in teaching the child to be aware and to know where harm is potentially coming from and what to do to avoid it. The child will carry such knowledge and nurture it to empower another in turn. There are thus essentially two types of facts – those which disempower and those which empower.

If a person is walking upon bad quality paving stones, their paths are unstable. This can be uncomfortable and dangerous, terrifying and precarious, and so the emphasis must be on the security of the 'facts' people walk on. Many people are walking on poor quality stones. Some people don't build anymore. They remain at a standstill, and they know they are safe because they have been there a long time. This is their choice, however, and they may do as they please on their journey.

The price of regaining the power over one's self is to release the idea of having power over anyone else. However, the problem with this idea is that some people have never had a sense of their own power apart from their power over others. All people would be completely equal.

Controlling People Using the Words of Belief

Whoever defines the language of belief has power over people's internal and external lives. It is often those in positions of authority who define them. Theirs are the voices with microphones. And as such definitions are also commonly defined by force. These are the people with the readiest access to such violence, be it physical or mental or spiritual. The rich and powerful, with their privileged influence over the sources others use for information – be they television or films or radio or any of the other mediums that form the veins of the human race's metaphorical body – are able to promote their own particular ideas. The promoted information will then be used to construct humankind's collective and individual pathways. These people with power can never be wrong: they define what is wrong. All that matters is who has the loudest, most powerful, and most far-reaching voice, for this is what establishes which ideas of truth and goodness are accepted and which get side-lined. Words are reduced to prostitutes to the powerful and rich; 'peace' is just a coin in a rich man's pocket.

Yet even within each person words can change meanings without changing labels. Pathways can be long, twisting and hard to walk on when one accepts a faulty groundwork for them. But nobody can learn what is right for them without finding out what is wrong for them. It is important to forgive mistakes. Mistakes are lessons in disguise. Yet with humans' polarized notion of truth and lies, if a person finds out they have been walking a way that is wrong for them, or have laid stones which were not strong, the only option is to go from believing you were 'right' and doing 'good', to the polar opposite of feeling everything has been 'bad' and 'wrong' and 'untrue'. This is cruel. It dismisses what they have put effort into as something that wasted time or led a 'bad' way.

This makes it hard to change direction. To ask people wholly to abandon their previously held truth is to encourage people to be unwilling to change at all, to grip tightly to their previous ways and get defensive about any idea that has not seemed to work as they desired.

It is the polarity in human words that makes change so unappealing. If one sees the truth as akin to a destination on a pathway, with slopes, and bends, and one simply makes a turn as opposed to abandoning the previous pathway, the concept is gentler. The uncompromising attitude which results from human's use of words does not affect only people's relationships with one another, but also people's attitudes toward their own choices, and their wider relationship to their own self. People change incessantly, but the terms 'truth', 'good', 'right', 'holy' and so on actually discourage the opening up of this process.

Yet the combination of being discouraged from changing, together with the ability to reconfigure the definition of words so they do not need to change, forces people to continue down their pathway without ever truly directing it. The only time they can do so is when disaster strikes, or when something takes place that is utterly unbelievable according to their current way of living and thinking.

In individual lives this can be seen in the way a religious person can lose faith after a relative or close friend dies suddenly, or a scientific person 'finds God' and feels that they had missed the whole reason for living before that time. The point is that beliefs are formed by facts, and the facts at such individuals' disposal have suddenly changed. They perhaps were not 'wrong' before.

Thinking back to those two people sitting in a room, another key reason is clear as to why their discussion of beliefs was potentially more confrontational than talking about the weather. The problem is not just with the terms one uses when describing their belief – it lies also in the beliefs themselves.

What characterises the words used to describe belief, namely their broadness and polarity, is not distinct from the belief systems themselves. It is worth noting that in terms of chronology, attitudes come before words. The attitudes exist and create the need for words to describe them. To better understand why this way of portraying beliefs has come about, one should perhaps look at the environment in which such beliefs were formed.

Taken back to the earliest stages of human interaction, ideas would have been constructed in isolated environments with no prior conception of life. If someone then felt that he or she had important understandings of human existence, this person would have been the first in history. Therefore, these first ideas would have been communicated to a world which, metaphorically, was a blank canvas.

A group of human beings may have decided that someone had an idea which applied to more than just the individual. Alternatively, a set of beliefs may have been worked through together. As human populations moved out of isolation, they would have found that there was a limit to how far they could spread their beliefs, because as their borders expanded they met other people who had their own picture already painted on their own particular canvas. And here was the thing: it was a different picture. At such a startling discovery, they would have had two distinct options – they could decide that one is 'right' and the other 'wrong', or they had to change their definition of what they had initially thought, and see it as just one idea among many ideas, and not as the only one.

Coming from a different area geographically and philosophically, the tribe would have had their own way of thinking for a long time, and they would not have known any other way of thinking of the world. It would obviously seem that alternative ideologies were inaccurate.

In this way one can see how the idea of polarity came into being: once an idea was established in isolation, and then moved out of isolation to meet another which was not like it, there came into existence words which reflected the judgements of the people responding to these revelations. An understanding of the world made in isolation came up against perceptions that challenged or contradicted it, and therefore, one must be 'right', and the other 'wrong', one 'good', the other 'bad', and so on.

Evolution

Creationism is the belief that divine beings have created and designed the universe. Some creationist stories reflect beliefs in space and time, and others involve plants or animals. For example, the Hindu idea of the world's formation involves a lotus flower and Brahma emerging from within it.

There has been much discussion to define and translate all of the terminology which is used in Holy Scriptures. There is an obsession with the specifics of time: many people are governed by time in their world. Other religions do not discuss the definitions of Tuesdays and Wednesdays. Inuits say that the bird god they called Raven created the world. Aboriginal stories say all the ingredients of existence were within the Earth and that it was born in a moment of Dreamtime. Chinese philosophy speaks of yin and yang – the forces of light and dark – as being the natural sources of things: the sun is created from yang and the moon is created from yin. There are many more ideas about the world's creation and they sit uneasily alongside that of scientific theology.

Science talks not of raven figures or lotus flowers. Yet without the separation between them which is produced by linguistic terms, the religious theology of 'God' and the secular worship of 'life' would be closer. Science could be the study of the divine in its purist form.

As a result of the development of technology it has long been possible to investigate the universe independently to ancient Holy Scriptures. Findings contradicted almost all creationist ideas about the origin of the human race. Scientific research into the universe's formation suggested that the world had been formed over a longer period of time than a matter of days, and with very different means – namely the mutation of initial bacteria.

The theory was called evolution. This theory clashes directly with the religious concepts of divine forces creating the universe. Some would say that ancient ideas of creation are mythology, while other ideas are religious doctrine, which means something different. One is Holy, while the other is a fictional interpretation of what was around the various races and peoples who were in existence.

Yet with the onslaught of science into religion's territory in the human psyche, there is to some people a blur between the two terms. In order to recover from the evolutionary theory that the Earth is a planet which developed independently of a creator, the religious interpretation of texts has been shifted. Previously, the religious accounts of the world's creation were thought of as the total truth. Some still hold this to be the case. These people are fundamentalists. Yet even head Church leaders ask that followers interpret some parts of holy texts as metaphorical. This makes any possible distinction between myths and all major religions completely redundant. It produces problems for both reactions to the world's changes: the reading of holy texts as facts renders them fallible whilst reading them as metaphors renders them as fictional as their now museum-bound predecessors. It is difficult to know which terminology to use: it can change among people.

How these deities created the world is crucial because if the validity of the sources that are available vanishes, then so too does the complex ideology which is built around the idea of that being's power. In short, chaos ensues if sacred texts which are describing the formation of the world differ from that which another source puts forward. It cannot be questioned that the religious text might not be true. If all religious texts are not true then God is a figment of the imagination which is not true at all.

When there are substantial findings that contradict Holy Scriptures it becomes hard for people of faith to adjust to the information. Rather than find the discovery worthy of respect, some people see it as an affront to them. They may attempt to defend their beliefs about life and God.

It is a tricky time in history. It is always necessary to adjust to new information that comes along. The ability to evolve with new ideas ensures the protection of humanity's progressive attitudes and identity: people are trying to find the truth. They are not simply defending the untrue out of habit. The defence of beliefs when necessary is also honourable, though. If a person truly believes in the essence of a religion they will try to defend those beliefs.

The alternative to dismissing new findings or abolishing old belief systems is to adjust humanity's current ideas of the divine. But some say that if the belief can be re-defined at any time then what is the purpose of defining it in any way at all? These people are known as religious fundamentalists, with exactly the same right to opinions as any other human being on the planet, and are no more left-field than any scientist saying humankind is a highly developed species which is related to apes. Both of these people can start a war. Both extremes can produce love. It is a choice as to what they create in life.

People put emphasis on the creationist aspect of divinity because they understand the notion of cause and effect: humankind is here for a reason, whether it is because of chance or divine destiny, or something in-between. If people could find out what the creative force behind their lives and the universe is, perhaps then it could increase their ability to live happily.

This is the difficulty: there is nothing with which to replace existing belief systems. Global culture is in many ways dependent on the thought that sacred texts were authentic and that the deities are real.

Scientific thought claims that the universe is all interconnected matter, with all its individual pieces related to and interacting with each another. Nothing is separate. In the basic sense, people eat, drink and inhale parts of the environment, and parts of the world's ecosystem eat, drink and inhale all of the output from these processes. In a wider, less naval-gazing sense, the world is made up of atoms, all vibrating and moving, and they are always able to change form. The universe is constructed of the same elements in various forms and conditions. It is the same substances in different states.

In this sense all the separate individual parts of life are really parts of one body. Matter or the physical universe, and therefore life itself, is actually one body, mutating and re-shaping with time. Therefore, in order to look at life properly it is perhaps useful to look at everything within it as a part of it. Rather than looking at aspects of the world as tables or flowers or elephants, one might see everything as merely what it is: parts belonging to a whole.

God must therefore reside within everything, for God is said to be always with a person. If in splitting an atom a nuclear explosion results, then the idea that God is always with one is perhaps emphasised, for it proves that to divide any part from itself is unnatural. 'God be with you'.

The idea that human beings are all so physically related to other creatures and that life evolved according to the laws of the universe can ostensibly seem to contradict the concept of an inventor – but this is not so. Top scientists endorse the prospect of a divine element in life, and say the more one studies the universe, the more this encourages awe for it. Albert Einstein was one such ingenious scientist who had a merged belief in scientific principle and divine contemplation. He admired the workings of a matter which was not without design.

It might not be so ridiculous to think that there is some form of design to the universe, given the wider universe and its wonder. It takes a phenomenal amount of faith in particles and elements to believe given any amount of time that they can form a universe.

There is a group of solar systems, linking clusters of matter around points of light, which burn for millennia, and this causes the particles around these points of light to vibrate at increased speed. The heated particles then become, after some cosmic mutations, human beings. The scientific belief in an arbitrary universe is a leap of faith perhaps even more acrobatic than the religious view.

One

The idea that there is only one thing – matter – shifting shape according to the forces of time, pressure, gravity and the physical laws of the universe means that words separate the inhabitants of the world once again.

A rock does not seem like it is alive, but to look at it under a microscope is to see that it is teeming with life, whilst looking at the Earth from a distance would render individual people completely undetectable. If billions of years were speeded up and were watched, it would be visible to see how active all matter is – one would see a sun bursting into life, bits of rock being dragged into its orbit, those rocks developing ecosystems and life-forms, and then on each rock lots of things mixing together, with the different conditions creating alternate results. It would be very easy to see the whole process as a single thing, especially if one was not involved in it, but merel watched.

The first mistake of most belief systems is that they come from a human perspective. Therefore, they divide the universe into two categories: the human and the non-human. This results in a perspective that is very much like the geocentric idea that the Earth was the centre of the universe and everything revolved around it. Humans are not the centre of the universe, or even the world, just as the Earth is not the centre of anything at all; the more humankind learns of the outer universe, the more this is realised.

The truth is humankind is simply a part of a big picture. Anthropocentrism results in the excusing of the destruction of the planet, the environment and other animals because of the view that non-humans are other, and therefore are seen as exempt from love and protection.

This way of thinking renders the human race ignorant of its place in the world: the perspective is about 'now' and about 'humans'. Thus humans are a self-obsessed, short-sighted species. If human beings are to be a more successful species, they need to start to care for the world as a whole.

People are raised to think of the entire world as a pompous actor thinks of his stage, believing that every line he speaks is utterly riveting, and that everyone is totally enriched at just watching him. Yet the world is not a stage, it is alive too, and some people miss the lines skies or animals speak because with their thinking that they are inanimate and have nothing to say, people render themselves deaf. Nature is not for walking on, but to be enjoyed and listened to, as a crucial and eloquent part of the play.

There is a sense of intelligence to life which does not encourage the attribution of nihilism and worthlessness to it at all. Rather, it produces the perception that perhaps higher forces are at work. This is the basis of the religious idea: that God is in control of everything. If 'God' is in control of everything, then whether the wind or the rain or gravity creates everything, or 'God' does, there is no difference. God is in every atom. The all-seeing I.

Yet God is often placed in other realms such as the afterlife. The idea of an overseer is suggested by many religions, an assessor; it is said that when a person gets to the after worlds they will meet God and be judged. But if God or the divine beings are purely separate, they would not be able to know what everyone is thinking and doing. Divine power would be somewhat limited. If God were only in Heaven then the deity would have no idea about how 'good' or 'bad' a person is, and would not be able to admit or deny a follower access to the good or bad afterlife with the authority befitting the post, for example. Therefore, a divine omnipotent being cannot be absent, and if it is not absent, it is right here, right now, and if it is right here, right now, this is it.

God is the Alpha and Omega, the up and the down, the light and the dark, but not in outer space. In such a definition of God as being within all things, everywhere, but nowhere separate, atheism and theism start to seem like merely words splitting hairs: one says I believe there is no such thing as a divine force moving through everything, and one says I believe there is – but no matter what, all is the same only with different words used to describe it.

The separation of God and all that is, the idea that people are answerable to an external realm or being, observed and cared for by it, makes it seem like they have no need to care for one another or do anything themselves. Yet if God is everything that exists, then how people treat all that is here now is certainly and undeniably the way that they are behaving towards the deities.

If God is older than time, omniscient and all-powerful, it makes no sense that religions claim that some are excluded from God's love. Religions' claims that those outside of its grasps are an accident or even a stain on the face of God's planet seem to be flawed.

Another separation which is often suggested by words is that you are not part of this omnipotent being; that you are somehow separate and must get back to being a part of it, of being acceptable to God. Yet if God is all that is, being separate is impossible, and everyone is always part of the whole of God's care. It is impossible to be alive without God.

This negates another idea purported in religious ways of speaking: that God is special. If God is everywhere and everything, God is not special. God is the mundane and every day. Yet it is the highest statement possible if a person declares themselves a part of God: they have got back to where others want to get back to, and they must either be lying or have found the secret key to unlock the God door, and let others in too! The response has often been either to kill or to celebrate these people, but rarely just to shrug and say 'well, who is not?'

This shows that people are not listening to the messages of God. People are saying the divine being is only where they say it is, only loves who they say it should, and is powerless in many ways.

By separating God from humanity, one person from another, one species from another and the mortal from the divine realm, religious

119

thought seems to be claiming that God is elsewhere. The only way a person following an omniscient God can escape the implication that God resides in themselves (as well as their enemies and all of existence) is to declare that God is actually only partially powerful and can see a limited amount. This illuminates the one polarity which makes sense: either God is all-powerful or does not exist.

Just as religious beliefs distinguish humankind from the non-human world so they distinguish humanity from that which is the Holiest of the Holy – they separate humans from God. To see that every person is given the chance to be a part of God, life, or any other word we chose to use, is 'The Key'.

The Equality of All Things

The problem with saying God is everything is that this would include people's enemies as well as their friends. It is difficult. Many do not want to believe that God is in a murderer or a stripper.

Yet a person who murders may later 'find God' and become a perfect example of a holy person. Therefore, it is difficult that people suggest what God is and what God is not and who God is a part of and who God is not a part of and so on: people are always able to choose the better version of who they were previously.

On the other hand, someone watching a stripper may find it very easy to see God in him or her, while a very religious person may see the situation very differently. The difference between a murderer and a non-murderer, or a stripper and a non-stripper, often lies in the examples they have been shown. Clearly a person is affected by a series of different experiences, and if someone is exposed to violent images, comes from a violent home and lives in a country where it is legal to own guns, this is likely to result in a violent individual. If someone is raised in a loving home, with no exposure to guns or violence, he or she is very unlikely to grow up as a violent and abusive human being. It is not that killers are innocent. But if there are more moves to protect the young from exposure to violence then the idea that acts of violence are acceptable in society will be removed. Currently, humanity celebrates war heroes and condemns those who do the same acts. Murder with a uniform is protecting the country and innocent civilians. However, the messages are blurred.

The important thing to observe then is that all effects have a cause. Society must be conscious of what people are exposed to and the messages they are given. The acts are important but it is the intention that is the really important part – no one is saying someone who kills to protect is less than heroic, but it is the intention behind the action which makes them so and not the action itself.

If the televisions and media are saturated with violence and cheap ideas of sex, this will cause people, not necessarily 'bad' people, to act differently than if they have only been shown images of peace and love. The people who are more susceptible to negative messages of harm are most likely to be those who have been harmed previously. They have lost faith in helping others and the good, because that faith has been tainted by backgrounds such as violent homes or sexual abuse. Therefore, what those who judge these people are saying is that those in pain are only deserving of more trauma and rejection.

If someone is fortunate enough to be raised well, they have love and care which can help people back from the brink. But they are often brought up with attitudes that merely scorn them. The difference between them and what they are scorning is often simply the amount of pain the people have been through – they have merely had different information put into their systems about what is acceptable and what the world is like. In the same way that a physical wound may weep puss or blood, emotional wounds weep violence, pain and self-hatred. There is a cyclical nature to pain as people react to another's pain by giving them yet more of it, and no one can be healed physically or emotionally by being hurt over and over.

This attitude even extends to human self-assessment: people often judge themselves harshly for their desires, their 'sinfulness', just as they do to others. It is said people need to repress uncomfortable feelings and pull themselves together, which leads to low self-esteem and a paralysis of the emotional world within people. There is no right or wrong objectively, for people have invented the concepts on which such judgements are based. There is no right or wrong objectively, only what is right or wrong for an individual. The problem is not that 'bad' things happen in the world: humans decide what is happening. The power is within people, and people will always feel the consequences of all actions. There is no goal or destination, something to get back to or go towards, but an endless in-between state of lucidity and consequence. Cause and effect is all that there is, and nothing else.

Divinity can be made 'on Earth as it is in Heaven' if one only sees that there is no Heaven but here, and no Hell but here. God can only do what humanity does, given that It has 'no hands but yours, no feet but yours' (as the Bible states), and the power is in the hands of human beings.

As things stand, the portrayed separation of God and the physical means that if people are unhappy with something in their lives, they sometimes ask God to help them from afar. The power is not theirs, the effects people have on the world are not theirs: all that influences is elsewhere and out of human control, essentially. This is a cause of despair for people wondering why something awful has happened, or why salvation is not coming. Because they can feel as if they have done something to upset that which is elsewhere, or that they are somehow awaiting for some external source of guidance and help. They may agonize over what they should do or how they could please their deity.

Games played endlessly between different peoples are also played out within people's minds. This is an important reason why atheists consider the belief in God to be dangerous: it removes power and consequence from one's life, so one may either do what one wants and call it Holy Will, or never fulfil desires because of the feeling of awaiting someone else's actions or covert permission to act.

'God' and 'life' are similar terms in some ways. Yet this is not entirely accurate, and it risks closing the debate on what happens after physical life has ended. Theism states that there is life after death. Scientific doctrine says that the physical is all there is, and life ends with the body's cessation.

Again, these polar positions seem to discourage the investigation of any middle ground. Further polarity comes from what might happen after death should there be anything at all – most religious beliefs purport concepts of 'Heaven' for 'good' people and 'Hell' for 'bad' people. Given that everyone lies somewhere in the grey scale of good and bad, and all religions have a different definition of what 'good' and 'bad' might be, it is inevitable that this becomes a little confusing for everyone concerned.

Science generally believes that the physical is all there is, and that when that dies, people die completely and no part remains. Followers of this belief system criticise religious thinking for not accepting the 'facts' of this process of living and dying, but science itself will not accept facts which suggest anything more than this being possible. Scientists dictate answers by asking only questions which shape responses in their ideological favour.

For example, if the question is 'do living things die?' the answer is yes. If the question is 'do living things not die?' the answer is likely to be very different to the straightforward one of the previous phrasing. It is a very difficult area, death, and has no simple answers. The words 'dead' and 'alive' are a perfect example again of vague terms placed in a dichotomy, with the reality being endlessly in the grey. For example, a fifty year old man looks at a picture of his seven-year-old self. Is he looking at himself or a stranger? Is this seven-year-old person 'dead' or 'alive'? To say that seven-year-old is 'alive' would require the evidence of that exact child with his speech, body, outlook, desires. This is not possible. Yet to say the child is 'dead' is not true either, for he has changed, but he remains alive.

Almost every cell in that man's body has been replaced many times over in his life, meaning that even in a physical sense, he has 'died' many times over - yet 'he' remains. There is no magic line that gets crossed when one physical form 'dies' and the other is born. It is constantly being born and dying at the same time, and in this way, is really doing neither, because it is impossible to do both at once. Therefore, there is no such thing as death or life, but merely how one is now, what state a person is in now – life is not concrete, nor is it opposed by the idea of death, but all that exists is endlessly in a state of transition between shapes.

If there is evidence of life after death, it obviously is evidence for the existence of God in many people's eyes. This discourages science from investigating such a possibility, because it would be loath to give any sense of authenticity to any religious belief. The discussion of such ideas need not be so akin to two bulls locking horns. If there is life after death, it does not prove the existence of God; it proves only that there is life after death. If there is life after death, it would mean that human beings have souls – or Jiva or Atman or any other terms which are deemed to be more appropriate.

There is a considerable amount of evidence which is ignored by both parties that suggests a non-physical element to all living things. This evidence is sourced from three main areas: evidence of something prior to birth as a physical being, evidence of post-physical activity during the physical life, and evidence of some form of awareness after the cessation of the physical state. In all of these areas there is substantial evidence to suggest in the affirmative that, yes there is a non-physical element to living beings.

In the area of life before birth, theories of the existence of past lives have for millennia been evident. The evidence which supports the idea comes in several forms. Firstly, and perhaps most importantly, people claim to have remembered them. Some people have very distinct information, and young children have been said to recall events and specific details of previous incarnations with such accuracy that they can be traced to people in recorded history. For example, a young boy remembers details of a World War II lifetime, is able to name pilots and landing pads, plane types and where his aircraft was shot down. Others are born with wounds which match where people have sustained mortal injuries in battles, and have described the infliction of them in detail. It has then been possible to find the person who died with such an injury in medical records. Others have strong feelings of kinship with various countries, races of people, times or events in history. They feel like they were there.

Others are less sure. They do not claim to have any such feelings of familiarity, no unusual interests in certain times in history. Yet under hypnosis by professional psychiatrists, these people recall experiences of past lives. Coins found only in the back rooms of museums are described in precise detail. The dates of marriages are matched perfectly in databases. People mostly unconsciously recognise their own identities, perhaps!

Past lives could also explain why our identities are not simply genetic; family members and siblings vary wildly. Some say it is the nature versus nurture debate, but with siblings who are genetically identical there are still personality differences, and if it was the difference of nurture only then the differences in siblings would surely be proportionate. Yet the way in which criminals can have family members who are human rights activists, Christians can be related to prolific drug users and hippies are related to yuppies, suggests there is seemingly no limit to how varied people can be while having similar DNA and similar upbringings.

Some children are by nature volatile no matter what their peaceful parents do, while other children are calm and in the face of violent lives remain so. This suggests there is a factor beyond their genetics and their environment perhaps; some previous knowledge or experiences that they have been through. This evidence combined suggests the likelihood of experiences before a person's human birth.

In terms of evidence for a soul in living things during our current life, there is most concrete evidence as a result of Kirlian photography, or aura cameras, which capture the electromagnetic field around all living things. This includes plants, people, animals, and so-called inanimate objects. There are varieties of colours around all things, and when a person dies, it is claimed that there has been evidence of this presence rising out of the physical body. This can be related to the way in which a body loses an average of 7lbs of weight at the point of death for no apparent reason in terms of their physicality.

There are two types of colour shapes, or auras, which can be shown through Kirlian photography – the alternating aura, and the fixed aura. So-called static objects, such as chairs or shoes, have static auras, which do not change shape or colour regularly or extremely. People and animals, on the other hand, have changeable auras, can have many colours or few, and they alter according to moods and thoughts. This suggests there are non-physical elements to living things and that the non-physical element is affected by physical conditions.

The final form of proof for souls in living things is the arena of life after death. This includes the experience of living beyond death by people and then returning, and also the evidence of observing non-physical beings existing outside of the physical realm.

Firstly, many people have experienced some kind of paranormal activity, be it ghosts, inexplicable noises or changes in their environment which have no logical explanation in physical terms, and other such confusing experiences. It is not a secret underground freakish idea, but what many very logical and normal people have claimed to have experienced.

For the people who haven't, however, this is no evidence whatsoever. Photos can be forged they will say, sound clips easily simulated, and experiences misconstrued in people's minds. But the prolific volume of evidence should not be dismissed just because people have seen as they have seen and have not seen as another has.

If this means nothing, then perhaps it is a good idea to examine the experiences of those who have died and regained their lives. To be close to or actually clinically dead, and then to regain full consciousness later through artificial or miraculous means has elicited some interesting declarations from those concerned. They often claim they have had experiences of other realms and were not dead when their body technically was. These peoples' testimonies of life after death are commonly described as near death experiences.

Individual recollections range from feelings of calm and love to tunnels of light. There are some very unique, intense experiences. They have become increasingly common with the advances of modern medicine, as there has been more ability to revive people from dead or nearly-dead states. For several decades, scientists have looked into the area with some interest. This is because, unlike ghosts, the area of the near-death experience leaves scientists unable simply to smother the evidence.

This is due to one specific element of the experiences. After being officially declared dead, individuals are able to recall after regaining consciousness events that took place when they were not alive. With no brain activity, no pulse and no signs of physical life, these persons, after regaining consciousness, are able to explain things which others can verify happened on different floors of the hospital, or words that family members said to one another many floors down from where their body was at the time. Such situations are not rare or freakish, and cannot be explained by calling them 'delusions', 'misperceptions' or 'lies'. Without a brain decoding their sensory input, and with no heart to pump the oxygen which fuels the operation of ears and eyes, the only explanation is they were somehow able to hear the conversations and see the events with something other than their physical bodies. With this, the conclusion must be that there is a part of people which remains active after their physical death.

Put together, the evidence of life before death, non-physical elements to physical life as it happens, and of life after death, encourages the idea that the existence of souls in life is real.

The experience of past lives and post-death experiences leads to the idea of a reincarnation process. This is the idea that the essence of a living thing continues after death. It is a belief which says that the flesh is changed for the spirit in the same way that clothes are changed for the physical body. Reincarnation is a popular concept which has been around for millennia, and it is an important element of many of the world's religions and philosophies. For example it is a central principle of the majority of the popular Eastern philosophies, as well as the Norse and Ancient Egyptian beliefs among many others. It was also regularly discussed in the written works of the greatest philosophers of Ancient Greece such as Plato, Socrates and Pythagoras. It is one of the most lasting ideologies that the human race has envisaged as an understanding of life.

Given the problems with language, the prevalence of zero-tolerance theologies that do not acknowledge the possibility of a reincarnation system, and the resulting slow pace for any growth or expansion of beliefs, centuries keep passing without this idea being given much credence in the western world. Believers in this process of life simply await the collection, like the precursors of geo-centrism or hand washing, of enough evidence to make it embarrassing not to believe it is a reality.

If, and some say when, it does, there will be a tremendous upheaval in the standard western ideas of science and religion, and neither want this to happen: both are insisting they know what they are doing, and in their current forms what they are doing either involves spirituality of a single-life kind, or atheism in the same finite vein of theology.

There is therefore no welcome mat laid out for such a revolutionary introduction to all global thinking. Reincarnation is to science what evolution is to religion. Given that the scientific thinking of atheism or agnosticism is an informant for others such as capitalism, consumerism and ego-driven ideas of accumulation and the self as the focus of all life, there is a huge stack of cards which will have to fall should all people begin to believe in reincarnation.

The irony is that the chaos which is caused by not acknowledging reincarnation is much more extreme than anything which could result from accepting it. Many of the questions which torment people currently could find answers. For example, why do people suffer, why are people cruel to one another, what is the purpose of life, and many more questions which are impossible to answer without the concept of reincarnation becoming evident.

Those who believe passionately in it could perhaps argue that not believing in the process of reincarnation is akin to not believing in oxygen. In this sense, oxygen and reincarnation are both ideas which have plentiful evidence. We can also in some ways perhaps see the effects that each has on people's lives, both individual and collective. They are both more or less transparent forces which require extreme focus or the use of special cameras and technology to observe. But the one crucial difference which makes believing in oxygen easy and believing in reincarnation less so is that believing in the existence of oxygen does not challenge pre-existing belief systems, and therefore the gain is much and the cost little, whereas believing in the existence of reincarnation would require us to expand on our current belief systems.

Of those who have not looked into studies of oxygen, yet believe it exists anyway, why do they? They do so because people are told it exists and because we feel ourselves breathing. In light of the evidence discussed, it would appear that we also feel a lot of the causes and effects of reincarnation, but, particularly in the Western world, we are told there are other reasons for these things and so often dismiss these features of our worlds as something other than the results of the reincarnation process.

Yet to the people who believe in reincarnation it seems we still feel ourselves 'breathing'; it seems clear. Those who believe in reincarnation may feel there will come a point in time when it is understood all over the world that all life is reincarnating; that a person takes all that they do and say and feel, with them. People will, according to reincarnation theory, never be able to fully escape the clutches of their essence, and would not perhaps want to should they know what is there.

Will

The will of nature is what makes a grain of grass grow toward the sky, a lamb walk or a bird fly. The other form of will is that of the mind, which has all kinds of desires as a result of information from external senses.

The separation is very evident between natural will and the mind's will, but there is an interaction between them, as with all things: the way a person thinks of feelings effects one's interpretation of their emotions and sensory experience. For example, a person may interpret their own elation at accumulating great wealth as evil and conversely, a person may argue that the joy would not exist without an intellectual awareness of what the notes with royal faces printed upon them could bring, for they are in themselves completely meaningless. This shows how intellectual structures effect interpretations of external and internal experience.

It is true that animals without the mental capabilities of humans display immense awareness of their environment and one another. For example, dolphins have been known to rescue humans from shark attacks, with no benefit to themselves. There are numerous instances where people have explained how their dog has saved them from attack, and so on.

Dramatic instances occurred during the Indian Ocean earthquake Tsunami which took place in the year 2004. Here, fascination was provoked by the way in which although an estimated 270,000 people lost their lives, almost no animal bodies were found. Some witnesses reported that animals had fled the site of the Tsunami prior to any lethal events. There were reports of elephants screaming and running for higher ground, dogs refusing to leave for their usual walks on the beach, flamingos abandoning low-lying breeding areas and zoo animals hiding and refusing to come back out. Some say it was because they had felt the vibrations in their feet and have better senses of hearing than us. However, they could not possibly have known what was going to happen or have worked out a pre-planned strategy for survival. Furthermore, if it was purely their physical senses that they were responding to with their actions, they would have all had similar reactions: running, acting strangely and hysterically, panicking haphazardly. There was method to their responses, however, as shown by the effectiveness of their actions.

Traditionally, scientists believe non-human species are less able than humans. Almost all species of the animal kingdoms are generally aggressively relegated in psychological and emotional status. Yet on the evidence of such experiences, one could easily claim the opposite: they are more able than human beings to perceive their life and environment's conditions. Suddenly the tables are turned in terms of who is stupid and who is not.

The missing fact here is that people, too, are animals. In saying sometimes that non-human animals are less capable than humans and at other times saying they are more capable is in both cases missing the point: other animals are not less competent than human beings, nor more able than human beings – they are exactly like human beings.

The difference is primarily one of intellectual capability, which has been raised to be the apex of life as human beings understand it to be. Humans have watched how their supposed intellect ability led to the dominance of all other species. People therefore understood it to be of the greatest value, and the crucial part of the human experience.

It is true that advancements in intellectual capabilities do dramatically improve the lives of those lucky enough to be exposed to knowledge. People's education can change their lives, and most of the class systems of the world rely on the exclusivity of their elitist education systems to sustain their positions of superiority and authority.

In the midst of this feelings are once again laid by the wayside as things not of worth. Animals have in general less mental capacity than humans, and are more likely as a result to live by their feelings about life. The way in which most animals are more able to perceive and respond to threat than humans in some ways, suggests feelings are not as useless or interconnected with the mind as a few human teachings declare and are perhaps operating with a superior sense of themselves.

Scientific accounts of feelings claim that they are a release of chemicals from the brain as an output of stimuli from the body. For example, a hand is held over a flame and nerve endings in the skin send electrical signals to the brain which interprets them as a problem. Chemicals are released which encourage the muscles to want the pain to stop and so the individual will remove their hand in an instinctual response. This idea of emotions as simply cause and effect mechanisms is used to explain that they are an evolutionary function alone.

Illogical feelings, which are more complex, are explained in identical terms. For example, love is said to be at least a partial response to pheromones, which are released by each human and are translated by the brain to decipher whether another person will be good for breeding and is attractive to them.

In the sense of feelings as part of a physiological mechanism, it gets harder to explain how, for example, a person falls in love with someone who is clearly not good for her or him, or when love simply leaves a relationship even when no children have been born to satiate the supposed physiological incentive.

It has been experienced by countless human beings time and time again that when passion disagrees with logic, there is often only one winner. The very way that you can have a separation of emotion and the mind suggests that they are separately sourced aspects of one's being. A scientist might explain this by arguing that the body has decided that a person has physical properties which have been decreed to be attractive, but the mind is disagreeing on principles not understood by evolutionary survival mechanisms.

Therefore, there is more evidence of a debate over which is in control and should be listened to – the mind or the feelings of the body? The two key institutional ways of believing about life, scientific and religious perspectives, are linked on this point. Both do not believe feelings are to be considered a central way of governing decision-making, and that they should be repressed and ignored.

The way in which the animals of the Asian Tsunami used a combination of physical senses and emotional intelligence whilst not understanding what was happening intellectually, illuminates the way they use feelings to guide them. It suggests two key things: firstly, that feelings and the mind are not separate, but are interactive, and so choosing one over the other is impossible, and secondly that it is not necessary completely to understand a situation to know what to do. Put briefly, it shows that emotions are not simply responses to environment or stimuli, but are coming from a perceptive ability external from, yet connected to, the mind.

The idea of a conflict between the mind and the body encounters a problem, then: if experiences are coming from a place beyond intellectual comprehension, but from separate sources, where are these sources? It indicates that the body either has an intellectual element itself, or that there is a third element to the human being.

If the animals were feeling their way to safety, and those feelings are more than simply responses to the physical but have an awareness of their own, this could explain why they are so adept at surviving. Their feelings are more aware than physical senses which merely input data.

This may not seem convincing for some. Perhaps it is wise to look at other species with other examples of abilities beyond what their thinking could permit. There are many examples which reinforce the idea that feelings are intelligent, and operate not only as reactions to chemicals released by the body.

Magnetic termites are one such example. Found in Australia, these creatures are 5mm long and have a brain the size of a pin-prick, yet they live in heat-conditioned mounds which can be up to ten metres tall. They have one distinguishing feature, which is that they are always angled perfectly with the sun's pattern of rising, with flat faces aligned east to west for optimum sun exposure.

They are aligned north-to-south precisely, and the clusters of them found around the north Australian landscape resemble the stone circles of prehistoric peoples. This was clearly not done with their minds, as they are completely unable to digest the kind of geographic information that they would need to build these structures. They are not passing the information down. They have the ability already inside them, live outside of the brain and yet create things their brains alone would not be able to.

Thus, in putting the pieces of information together, clearly feelings can alert people to danger, and can give a person intuitive knowledge that a mind would not be able to, potentially enabling human beings to live more evolved lives than a brain alone could perhaps provide.

If this does not convince people that feelings are intrinsically capable of information transferral, there is more for nature to explain on the matter. The key point is that brains are not the only answer: the limits they have are such that people can only understand so much with the power they offer, yet with other parts of the human being the knowledge is greater.

For example, the human heart has an electromagnetic field which is 5,000 times more powerful than that of the brain, and the amount of electricity the heart generates is 100 times greater. This shows just how much more forceful the power of people's hearts are in comparison to brains.

However, what is more interesting is the idea that rather than a battle between heart and mind, there is something more still: energetic wisdom. The wisdom of life that is present without the brain's or the heart's influence can perhaps be proven by looking at creatures which have neither a brain nor a heart. For this point, it might be worth looking at what are called the Hado experiments. Hado is an area of study involving the characteristics and qualities of ordinary substances such as rice and water. What it has found is that substances without brains react to intentions and messages, for example language, when directed towards it. Decomposition increases and decreases speed according to how loved a substance is, and water changes its molecular shape as a result of messages spoken to it.

The Hado experiments, done in several languages, all resulted in the same decomposition changes according to the specific verbal and written messages given to the substances, such as "I love you" or "I hate you". This indicates several things. It suggests that human's words hold energy, and that the energy is communicated universally, whereas the words are only intelligible to those who understand the syllables. These atoms could not understand language; they understand the energy behind language, and therefore understanding resides not in the brain alone.

This has phenomenal consequences in several ways: these substances demonstrate the ability to emote, clearly demonstrating the division which exists between emotion and the mind; love makes these beings happier and healthier, and when something is communicated, it is understood by other things which clearly know not the words' meaning. This shows that it is the feelings, of which words are representative symbols, which are the key to communication; in other words, that words are symbols of energy behind them.

This is worrying to humanity's current way of thinking and treating things. Some people suggest words do not matter, and are unimportant. They say what a person views on a television or in the movies has no effect on anything at all really, despite spending millions of dollars on advertising. In the light of these understandings, humans appear unfathomably ignorant of their actions. Understanding is not in the mind alone, but in a human's actual being. Even water can understand what has been put underneath it in writing or spoken to it in voice; so of course the acts of hatred which are put on television screens and spoken through people's mouths have an impact on the wider world!

When putting all this information together, there are wider implications: everything has a form of consciousness, from the Earth, the sea, plants and fish. Each and everything has awareness. All matter matters. This is akin to Gaia theory: the idea that the world is a united organism.

The way that thoughts are placed above feelings is a small symptom of a wider distress for humankind: dislike of its own nature. No other creature on Earth has a problem with their natural state: if a person were to live as he or she feels alone, she or he is living according to their nature, yet they are likely to meet much disapproval should they attempt such a thing. In most of human society it is impossible to do exactly what one feels one would like to do. Acts such as sex, nudity and the bodily functions – even at the elemental level of human experiences – are, varyingly, said to be evil, dangerous, or repulsive.

Human philosophies often hate humankind with a passion. Whether it is because humans are displeasing to God in their nature or because of Adam and Eve's acts in the Garden of Eden, the result is the same: many people endlessly feel shame about their natural desires, guilt and fear about themselves, and try to repress their emotions. In this way human life becomes a battleground of suppressed experiences.

Yet if one's emotions and desires are not truth, then what is? A person's emotions and desires and all the things thought of as negative in many ways are truer than anything else people are trying to replace them with, which is ironic: in pursuing truth humans are losing touch with their own truth.

Nature is the primary set of laws that matters or has any claim to being valid. This is because their examiner is time itself, which has no mercy for weakness. It is objective and does not favour that which threatens or smiles sweetly, and will test more intensely than any form of intellectual or spiritual interrogation.

Yet it is a fundamental hatred for the self and the planet that religions often implant through their notions of holiness and divinity. Why would a good God create something that was naturally evil? Why would the rest of the world be beautiful in following its own will and nature, yet humans be evil if they do? It divides humankind from its environment. It is an idea which makes nature dark and separated and says people would be doing the best thing by betraying it. The wrong is two-fold, in that it implies nature is something bad, and also that humans are able to sever themselves from their nature at all. Humans must learn that this is not desirable, and not possible. It's a self-destructive desire.

Fear of nature breeds falseness in society and individuals. It makes life unbearable; a constant grind between how people are and how people are told they should be. Naturally, the result is that humans are unhappy as collectives and individuals.

The only outlook which encourages hatred of natural processes is that which sees all of life as wrong. This would be a choice a person is making, as much as to see the world as good would be, and any perspective which lies between these two absolutes.

Yet whether people see the world as good, bad or okay, it exists, and how people interact with it affects them. Therefore, to make a working system is paramount, and if humans do, surely then life itself would be a better thing to have? People have a tremendous ability to effect life, and this is different to plants or most other creatures.

The human will is important to the species' survival as well as other life forms. So if humans choose love and health, it must begin with them. People must love themselves. Natural instincts are a person's basic essence of life, and the platform from which they construct all of their experiences in life.

Living according to nature is humankind's best hope for making the foundation of the species strong and also allowing people the chance as individuals to remain somehow in tune with themselves.

It is the closest humanity can get to objectively knowing any creator's intention for its creation: the way it has been made to be. If people look at the world, one of the most compelling reasons for there to be a God is its sheer perfection. It all works so perfectly it must have had a creator, say many: every hand has a hand to hold, and the proof that feeling is the way forward, and that doing what is natural is less harmful than not, comes from looking at the way the world has been made. This world was not formed by thoughts or essays. There was no desire, pay-off or enticement with ideas of eternal reward: it just is. It naturally is, and the way everything else survives is by following feelings, with the reward being the emotion of joy. Logically then, emotion seems an instinct for survival.

It is unclear what the gain might be from believing humans to be evil vermin who must be taught divinity. Yet given that the nature inside people is seen as shameful, it is an insult to speak of a human as an animal. Animal instincts are very much rejected by some people and very few cultures or philosophies have survived which celebrate nature. This is perhaps because they were not able to compete with people who would abuse nature to progress and build their societies. Living in balance takes awareness, and respect. It is to see everything as being one, together.

People may want to have power to be great, but given the choice most would prefer to be admired, as opposed to forcing others to serve. People may want to have lots of wealth and luxuries to enjoy, but in the best sense it is not because they want to leave others with nothing. Some may want to have sex with many people. Yet not without consent, for it is likely that they want to love someone and have someone to love them.

It is no surprise, in terms of evolution, that these are exactly the activities which keep humans alive and have caused them to develop as a species; repressing and denying these aspects of human nature is almost suicidal.

The simple solution to this is to start feeling as well as thinking. By definition life is naturally able to sustain itself and so must be allowed to do so without the obstruction of falsely intellectual constructs.

The part of humans which is not of the physical realm has a voice to communicate. An energy which will always exist in varying places and times will have no language of the tongue or throat: would an eternal universal language be English, French or Mandarin? It can be suggested that emotion is the language of the eternal part of us, and speaks with a voice not of the physical Earth realm; when you die, it will live. It is the natural emotion, intangible but present, which should help humankind to understand its own desire.

It is natural to exchange love. If a person is without love, then he or she is often unhappy. To love is to know why people exist.

Love is the source of life - even in terms of the physical nature of reproduction. If one is loved and loving then it is astonishing what occurs. The existence one has felt yesterday can then become something more today. This is why many people say they have a broken heart if the person they are in love with leaves them or dies: love is the key to truth and happiness.

People are innately designed to give away all kinds of love, joy, peace. It is said by many theologies that part of the reincarnation process is karma. This is the concept that humans' actions are returned to them, and that what people cause another to experience they will eventually experience themselves.

It makes sense that among physically and spiritually intertwined parts, there should be a physical and a spiritually intertwined system of judgement. If all particles are able to shape themselves according to the environment, they have the ability to react to more than physical conditions, and existence moves two ways: ways a person feels internally as well as sees.

The rules of the physical world keep particles 'in place', as people understand the universe to be. The non-physical world has to be understood as well. It could be that in atoms and elements there are sets of interactive abilities which form the laws of the universe. If this were the case, reward and punishment would be an ongoing process of administration.

Karma is an idea that supports the concept that life is united, that there is a natural process in the midst of life. Everything interacts.

There must be a set of rules and an intrinsic interactive unity for the spirit, corresponding to those for the physical side of life.

The Law of the Conservation of Energy suggests that this is happening in the physical world. Energy works by transferring from one form to another. For example, energy transfers from kinetic energy to electrical energy. Yet it does not lose the original power it had. In this sense, Karmic Law is a spiritual concept reflecting the dynamics of the physical into the spiritual dimension.

Buddhism refers to a state it calls 'enlightenment'. Interpretations of the word are varying, however. Some say that it is a linear progression which culminates in the arrival at a place of perfect love and others that it is to be in the presence of love eternally. Some say that it is a circular process by which one could begin again if one chose to.

It is a concept of the Earth, a word, and describes something which is only partially of this world. The process of enlightenment which is partaken in would perhaps be the same throughout the universe. However, the word is not the 'being', the sensation, the act or quality, but simply a word.

The general consensus is that to be enlightened involves a lot of love. One is driven to find and to give love, and obviously it is at the centre of people's lives and experience of Earth. It also seems obviously to indicate the purpose of life on a deeper level. Given the law of karma and the joy which comes from receiving love, it seems a logical progression to unify the idea of there being a deliberate process happening in life and that to love and give love is the important part of life.

It is said that reincarnation is a system which is logical and linear. Yet those looking to understand it are, by definition, in the midst of the process itself. Therefore, the nature of the reincarnation process's destination is mysterious and questionable.

Someone who is reincarnating – i.e., who is alive – while claiming to know the destination to life is like a virgin describing sex. The analogy is a suitable one, given that sex is the origin of life. A three year old, however, does not understand and does not want to have sex. He or she would probably find it repulsive and would prefer to eat their food from a flying spoon whilst cuddling their soft toy. A child of six may want to play with worms but may also find another child attractive. A teenager may know what sex is but be a little afraid and would still like to play games. At a certain stage of development, though, people do not only become aware of fancying someone and the intimacies of sex, but also have the combination of the desire and the ability to fulfil their natural will.

This could be seen as very much like the process of enlightenment. Some are babies, gurgling but lacking autonomy, playing games and interested in bodily things. Some are like six year old investigating the world around them with curiosity. Some are like teenagers who look up from the floor and the toys and decide maybe they would like to experience more than before, and some are at the stage when they are able to experience unification with another. Although each person is on their own pathway, one will sense when the time has come to change their outlook on life, and most will be both terrified and joyful as they progress to the enlightened state.

Yet one doesn't mock a three-year-old for not wanting sex or having adult bodies. They are beautiful and that is the natural way for them to live. In the same way, it is sometimes the case that the spiritually undeveloped human would be disinterested in the contemplation of the eternal process.

Some souls are old, however. They are naturally wiser because of the amount of experience they have had. They may see through the superficialities and mirages of life that others are blind to. They do not need to be shown the existence of a soul, a past life or a sense of how to treat the people they adore. They have learnt these lessons and understand more than anyone can teach them. They may be able to understand a previous incarnation. They may be able to have an idea that there are other realms to life such as a spiritual world and even to be able to connect to beings and create from this place of wonder.

Alternate realities are demonstrated by experiences within the physical body. Out-of-body experiences are relatively common. Many of those who have a tragic accident say they leave their bodies for a period of time, watching from an alternate realm. Shakespeare even wrote in his most famous play, Hamlet, that "There are more things in heaven and earth, Horatio, than are dreamt of in your philosophy."

However, many religions state that a soul transfers from one physical form to another immediately upon the former's destruction. Some say it does not exist in-between its incarnations without a physical aspect. However, experiences such as out-of-body experiences suggest the spirit does not need a physical aspect. It is believed by some that spiritual places exist without the physical world's laws or structures. Although there may be various elements and regions to the afterlife -- as in the physical world – it does exist in some people's perceptions of existence.

The idea of heaven is shown by the experiences of those who have died and returned. Through the resuscitation of those whose brains and pulse have completely stopped it is clear that other realms have been experienced by many people.

A limitless sense of love and light is experienced by those returning from dead states, and those people range from highly religious people to atheists, from criminals to teachers. Their experiences are the best evidence people have about life's purpose.

The message from this divine realm is to love one another and the wider world, and this is exactly the message of 'The Religion of Self-Enlightenment'.

Love, joy and peace.

In time, there will be a pathway, peaceful and sloping, to eternal life, and nothing more; confusion will cease and all the mysteries of life which are yet to be revealed will be made clear and plain. The holiness which deities speak of will be mortal and angels will be you's and I's. Skies will be floors to other worlds, which will matter not because those here will understand the wonder of being here. Every moment will become then a precious gift without boundaries.

The exact spot one stands upon forever will be as a throne to kingdoms without divisions - kindred rulers will never be far from reach - and all will rest in peace, whether wakened or dreaming or both. Living shall be delightful for those blessed with its potential to experience their own charm. In this time, love and only love will be as rain to the deserts and sunshine to children.

SIXTEEN

Carrick had spent a lifetime on the book. He could not stop the overflow as he walked through cemeteries of doubt, dreaming of something more: of higher planes. His days in the hospital ended with him skulking halls while muttering under his breath theories of love, looking to ceilings for clarity and to his heart for awareness. Whether successful or not, he was trying these days to be a better and more alive person than in his previous life. It was all so unnecessary in the end, he thought - the answers were so obvious! It was the untangling that was the effort, of the things he had been told and the intertwined threads of emotions he had been ignoring. But he had done it now, and he took the manuscript to his nurse to ask how he could publish it somewhere.

"Miss Roberta, I've finished!"

"Well done, Carrick! How are you feeling? You've run your marathon, sweetheart!" she smiled.

"I don't know. Can I get it published? Ask me after that." Carrick had a contagious way about him.

"I've spoken to the head nurse about it and she says she'd be happy to send it off for you, dear."

And so it happened. At first, there was nothing. Then letters started arriving. First one, then two, three, four, all offers Carrick could not refuse. The head nurse, Jane Fisher, had asked around about it, being a helpful soul, and had sent it to several publishing companies. Carrick had a visit one day when he was in the shower and came out to find a man of forty-something years perched next to his bed. He looked terribly awkward but did not let that stop him from making a proud speech: "Hello Mr. Ares, my name is James Reynolds. I belong to a publishing company called Black Swans in London and we would like to offer you a contract to publish your book, err, The..." He checked his notes and spoke respectfully slowly: "Religion of Self-Enlightenment." Carrick had never heard the name read out like that before, and by such a well-dressed man.

It sounded beautiful.

"Oh yes," he said, in awe of his own blessings.

"We believe there is a big potential audience for this book. A book which blends all our modern confusions together as it does. It's just wonderful!" The man's happiness was dazzling Carrick by now, and he sat down on his bed to regain a sense of calm.

"Could you publish it right away?" Carrick asked, a little hurriedly.

"It will take a few months for it all to go through, but you will of course receive an immediate advance." He grinned, sleazily. Carrick accepted the deal and his book was sent away to decorate some trees. He was ecstatic! He was so happy! He laughed endlessly! The excitement of success helped in his recovery. He looked well, ate well, and slept well. He had something to look forward to.

A few weeks later his book was published ahead of schedule. The publishing house designed a book using an artist to add graphic illustrations of his words. This created a piece of writing that was Carrick's pride and joy. He had been jubilant when he saw the final edition, which looked something like the work of a latter-day William Blake, a real work of beauty and passionate endeavour.

Carrick was soon handed newspapers with reviews. He sat up in his bed to read, but his face sunk back down again. "The Religion of a Madman" read the headline: "A new religion by someone locked up in a mental institute – well, this reverses the usual stream of things I suppose, but do we really have to read it? Luckily, you are not a reviewer and are not paid to trawl through it but should you voluntarily do so you will find here a mix of science, religion and a quite nauseating positivity which is enough to make you go and join Mister Ares in his current place called 'home'. The last thing the world needs is another religion, especially one that caters for all. Good God, is there no escape?"

Carrick knew why – the publishing house had marketed the book with his personal struggle in mind.

SEVENTEEN

He stood, suitcase in hand, watching the scene as it fell into his past.

The nurses were all fond of him, greeting his departure coldly and wishing him well warmly. The fresh air then hit Carrick like a slap in the face from a pretty lady, and he smiled again. Don't worry, he told himself, don't worry. Do what you tell yourself and you'll be fine – listen to your heart. He'd been in a half-way house for the last few months and had set up a place to go when he got out with his book money. There was a sour taste to it all, though.

He tried calling the book company but was informed that the book had needed 'a twist' for the work to sell. They were sorry that he had not been told about it. It was not their intention that he found out that way. He felt betrayed and stewed over those calls. What had he done to deserve this? He sat down in his new and empty living room, and leant back to feel its rigidity and solidity. He decided he needed some furniture. He put his bags in the bedroom, and made a thoughtful note to get a new bed; he went to the kitchen to remind himself to buy some food; he felt irrepressible sorrow.

He left immediately. He felt strange and alone, searching the streets for a destination once again. He grabbed a coffee in a nearby café and sat there watching the skies move – the clouds passing each other by without even saying hello. His coffee was cold but he was too shy to complain, and so he held it like an impotent Houdini, willing it to be different than it was.

He stopped. In the eye-line of his cup, if he adjusted his sight as though he were doing a magic eye visual image, he saw a book. He recognised it immediately. And he was speechless.

'The Religion of Self-Enlightenment': someone was reading his book. Not just anyone, but someone who was clearly doing so by their own free will. They were in no way miserable as though they were trawling through yet another religious theory, but smiling at it! 'They' were tall and grey, about fifty years old and beaming with a healthy, wrinkled smile. The man looked happy. In that moment Carrick stared like he had just been shown a lost Renaissance masterpiece. Life had never felt like this before. Homes were still cold, coffee was still lukewarm, but his insides were glowing – things had changed in the outside world. Now, Carrick was an author! Carrick!

He had spoken from his inner world about something and had been heard. He briefly wondered how people can live without this feeling, just how they can fill the gap. But this was not his concern anymore, and the thirty years of experience with which he could answer that question rapidly slipped through the fingers of his mind, and gladly so: he didn't know anymore.

Carrick debated whether to go over to the man and indulge in his superstar moment! Maybe this could be his first book signing, he thought, and laughed. At the sound, the man looked up at him. Carrick apologized with a glance for disturbing his concentration and thought to himself, 'No, you can't offer your own autograph; it's just not the done thing. Maybe…'

And then suddenly Carrick had it. "That's an interesting title," Carrick began.

"Yes, it's an interesting book." Carrick melted.

"What's it about?"

"A new way of thinking about things. The guy's basically put together a thousand different things and made them all seem like they were always meant to be together. It's ridiculous! I really can't explain it, but it's good."

"You certainly look happy."

The guy shrugged it off and continued apace.

Carrick paused and looked around, realising he had not yet done the most obvious thing he could ever have had to do, and became gleefully excited, wheeling around in his chair to scan the street.

"Is there a bookshop around here? Maybe I could get myself a copy, seeing as it looks so enjoyable."

The guy looked doubtful. "Well, yes, there's one over the road, but you won't find any in there."

"Why won't I?"

"It's all sold out."

Carrick was glad he had spoken to this man.

"Where did you get yours?"

"I have my ways", he smiled.

"Didn't I read bad things about it, though?"

"Where? I've only heard good things about it, but I don't read the papers, so there you go."

The reader paused.

"Wait. Why did you act as if you hadn't known what it was about if you'd read about it?"

Carrick was stuck, and more words of truth squirmed like worms inside his mouth, desperate to escape the darkness of non-expression.

"Err..."

The wiggle, the strife, all audible! Yet several seconds of undisguised excuse-making on his part still preceded his answer.

"Well. Actually, I was merely being nosey. I wanted your opinion on it, see."

The man was not convinced.

"I know the author."

The look dropped to the floor and a smile rejoiced again.

"Really! Can I meet him?"

Oh no – it was one of those cases in which one lie falls into another.

"Well..." Carrick had presumed the reader would have backed away at this point, knowing that the writer was 'mad', and that he would be safe to continue lie-less. But then he realised his conversational partner had not read the reviews and genuinely wanted to meet him. Oh, the irony – the one time madness should have shielded him, it remained a weapon still.

"You know that he's mad?"

The face on the floor had a guest.

"Really?" He looked very concerned.

"Is he okay?"

"Well, no."

It wasn't the answer the older gentleman had expected. It was the truth. He looked sad, and clearly wanted to express some of his respect for the person who was responsible for what lay in his hands. He considered, and then conceded, "But that's why people write books, isn't it?"

The logic comforted his dear heart.

"Well, I guess so," said Carrick, the logic disturbing his own.

The café reader looked at his book as if it were the newspaper of its creator's world now, and then did something strange: he picked up his coffee cup and toasted misfortune.

"Here's to madness, then!"

Carrick felt humour return to a desert of seriousness. It was like a whole rainy season had fallen in one second.

"To madness... Ha!"

It made Carrick so happy. His coffee tasted hot! Over the next few days Carrick and the man met regularly in the coffee shop. Each day the man had new theories about what he had been reading. His name was Robert and he was fully employed as a cheerful soul, and redundant as a miserable, soul-sapped wage-slave. He and Carrick struck a chord immediately. Bob's humour cascaded onto Carrick, whose knowledge made him a semi-celebrity in his companion's eyes. Carrick told him that his name was Jonas – not because he was in the belly of a beast, but just because.

The respect he had for himself grew ten times more than if he had offered the man his autograph that first day. He understood the situation as a metaphor for life itself – that if you see yourself through someone else's eyes, and know they are not aware of who you are, you see yourself extremely clearly. Carrick had to hold back tears sometimes, intending as he did only to get to know the man, but feeling as he did so that he was getting to know himself again.

Indeed, life made love to him tenderly in exchange for those days of friendship. He had a friend and some money in his bank account, and he could not have asked for more. In fact, increasingly he had money in his bank account. He was soon not worried about checking his bank balance at all! He may write another book, he thought to himself, and maybe make it happier and more religiously-minded still! He laughed. The figures in his account rose.

Soon, the same people who had fobbed him off with bitter, patronizing common sense were calling him again with sugar in their voices. "Hello, Carrick!" "How are you doing, Carrick?"

He had lots of friends now! They would come round for tea and smile at his jokes and touch all the right places in their conversation.

Apparently the book was a success. The scoffing reviews changed when the people who actually bought the book started to make themselves heard. Carrick realised that newspaper and magazine editors were the biggest sheep of all and merely wandered astray because the shepherds of their readership were distracted most of the time. A review editor rang him and asked for an interview, and Carrick asked about the original notice in their publication. The editor apologised and said that because the book had the word 'religion' in its title he had given it to the religious section, which was staffed with devout believers alongside, to balance things out, a passionate atheist. Carrick considered that he must have been given the 'balanced' treatment then, according to this description. Lucky him!

Insulted, derided and on his way to being a huge success, Carrick turned the man down. But the editors kept calling, and offering bigger and better deals. Carrick was not a money man but it struck him that he could gather publicity and help people through his book. After all, it had taken a lot of suffering to get here; why should he turn down the pleasure part? So he began to accept the interview offers.

He did five until they stopped coming. Soon after, there was a rude bang at the door. It was raining and Carrick was feeling quiet and autumnal and was confused as to why someone would do such a thing. But it was Bob. He was holding a newspaper with the article on Carrick's book against the window pane. Carrick let him in.

"You're in the paper! You're in the paper!" He gasped. "Look!" and then read: "'My friend down the local coffee shop told me about the success initially, and I'm very happy about it.' That's you, isn't it?"

Carrick felt truly awful. Bob had said he didn't read the papers and Carrick thought that he'd be safe from this kind of situation.

"Bob, there's something I should tell you. I am in the paper, yes, but so are you. I'm the writer, Carrick, and you are the friend in the coffee shop." He waited for the response.

The rain just poured.

"Well, blow me down! It's you? I can't believe you lied to me!"

"I was shy about it and I didn't want you to know." It was too late. Bob was raving. But then he calmed down and accepted that what he had done was for a reason, and Carrick told him everything.

The next day, Carrick did not go to the coffee shop or venture out. He felt he had betrayed his friend. It wasn't that Bob was upset. It was Carrick who was upset, and he berated himself. He had already known that when you betray someone the real betrayal is to yourself. He felt bad that he had lied. There had been a couple of weeks of lying to Bob now, slightly too long to forgive, and only a day had passed since the confession, too short to forget. Carrick forlornly hiccupped sighs all afternoon.

Meanwhile, Bob waited at the coffee shop for his friend, the famous author, proud as a button. He decided to go round and bring him some cake and say that he hoped he felt okay; that he understood. Bob knew his friend felt awful for lying, but he was no longer mad at him after he found out why - we all make mistakes. He had always thought that if someone else makes an error, just remember that you have too, and then be gentle with them.

He did find it scary that Carrick had been certified insane. He could understand why he felt a bit shy about it. But even though they only met a couple of weeks ago, he knew Carrick well enough to know he would be beating himself up.

Knock and answer was the name of the game, but Carrick wasn't playing. Bob tried to get the window involved. He peered through but Carrick was nowhere in sight. "Carrick?" called Bob.

"Come on, Jonas. Don't be silly now, I've brought you some cake."

And Carrick answered.

Over the coming months, things died down on the fame front for Carrick. He settled into a quiet life, and then decided to move to California with his earnings. He wanted Bob to go with him but knew he could not. Carrick had a Green Card because his father was an American citizen, and had worked there for a year or two every now and then. He needed the sun, he said to himself, and smiled. He had not been in contact with his parents since he had been out of hospital, but leaving the country was probably a piece of information he could not really withhold from them.

He telephoned, his mum answered, and he cried. "Carrick, honey, we've read your book, it's in the papers, sweetie. We're so proud. We've been trying to find you frantically."

But Carrick could not stop crying and put the phone down. It rang back, and Carrick was glad, because he had not meant to hang up like that and felt bad instantly.

"Hello?" Carrick sobbed.

"Carrick, it's your Mum and I love you, where have you been? We heard you got out of hospital, are you okay?"

"Yes, Mum."

"Why don't you come for a visit? Or we'll visit you? Either would be great."

So Carrick went home. It smelt like home, it looked like home, it felt strange. But it was good to see his family. He felt lucky to have them, and told them so. His mother cried this time! He did not want to tell them about America, and found that he didn't actually want to go when he saw them. So he decided not to. He led a calm life in familiar London suburbs for many years, and moved to America at retirement age finally to get his rays of American sunlight. He bought a house by the beach where he could walk his dog and find calm in himself.

One day on his porch he sat back in his chair and fell into a sleep from which he was never to awaken. His dog barked, the moon looked pale, but Carrick was happy and well in no time, and all need to worry passed away. His eyes slipped down and hid his naked soul's modesty for the very last time.

He felt the same rush of light and love as he had before, he felt himself a being of beauty and love. But this time he knew that he had taken a bit of that beauty he had and planted it in the Earth, and because of that was content to leave it. His relatives, friends and soul sisters and brothers had been waiting, and they welcomed him back into their world. Carrick felt at home. Around him, as before, gathered an inescapable window into his existence, all the sadness he had been through, all the joy, all the hysteria. And then the questions came. Again, he was quietly asked:

"Have you learnt to love?"

And his spirit could not help but remind itself of the ease with which loving had been possible to him after acknowledging it to be life's only priority.

"Yes," he answered.

"How have you made the world a better place?"

And before him there appeared his trauma – his experience of having written his truth.

"I wrote a book. It was called 'The Religion of Self-Enlightenment'. I hoped that the world might love more, and that the people who read it would be able to give and receive their love with greater ease."

"Do you know how you affected people's lives? How you've changed the world itself?"

"No."

"Would you like to?"

Carrick considered this a while.

"Yes." He had done his best.

An image appeared, and Carrick saw how he had changed people's lives, young and old, rich and poor, happy and unhappy. He had made them a little sweeter and brighter. He watched them as their emotions changed, and regretted that he had missed this in life.

He had known his book was successful, and had appreciated it, but had spent much of his time keeping his pain quiet. Now once more a soul, he realised the error of his ways and apologised for having been so distant in his life. He then thanked that which had asked the question, and watched the world over his shoulder change its course by just a fraction at his hand.